Praise for the Wollstonecraft Detective Agency series

'An enjoyable plot, resourceful heroines, and fun writing'
— *Wall Street Journal*

'The telling is sprightly and vaguely reminiscent of
The Wolves of Willoughby Chase'
— *Financial Times*

'Smart and witty . . . Skilled illustrations and comical
narration and dialogue will charm readers thoroughly'
— *Publishers Weekly*

'Smart and clever girls will enjoy this refreshing mystery'
— *Kidsreads*

'Equal parts laughs and adventure, this lively mystery
will keep you guessing till the end!'
— *Discovery Girls*

'This is a winner'
— *School Library Journal*

'A must-read for fans of history, mystery and witty young
women, *The Case of the Missing Moonstone* is a charming
first instalment of what is sure to be a spectacular series'
— *Middle Shelf Magazine*

COMING SOON

The Case of the Girl in Grey

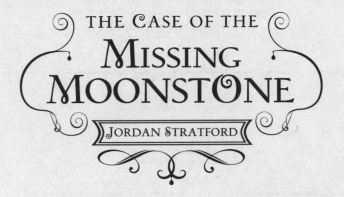

THE CASE OF THE
MISSING MOONSTONE

JORDAN STRATFORD

THE WOLLSTONECRAFT
DETECTIVE AGENCY

Illustrated by Kelly Murphy

CORGI YEARLING

THE CASE OF THE MISSING MOONSTONE
A CORGI YEARLING BOOK 978 0 440 87116 3

First published in Great Britain by Jonathan Cape,
an imprint of Random House Children's Publishers UK
A Penguin Random House Company

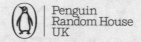

Penguin
Random House
UK

Jonathan Cape edition published 2015
This edition published 2016

1 3 5 7 9 10 8 6 4 2

Text copyright © Jordan Stratford, 2015
Interior illustrations copyright © Kelly Murphy, 2015

The right of Jordan Stratford to be identified as the author of this work
has been asserted in accordance with the Copyright, Designs and Patents Act 1988.

Penguin Random House is committed to a sustainable future for our business, our readers and our planet.
This book is made from Forest Stewardship Council® certified paper.

MIX
Paper from
responsible sources
FSC
www.fsc.org   FSC® C016897

Typeset in Guardi

RANDOM HOUSE CHILDREN'S PUBLISHERS UK
61–63 Uxbridge Road, London W5 5SA

www.randomhousechildrens.co.uk
www.totallyrandombooks.co.uk
www.randomhouse.co.uk

Addresses for companies within The Random House Group Limited
can be found at: www.randomhouse.co.uk/offices.htm

THE RANDOM HOUSE GROUP Limited Reg. No. 954009

A CIP catalogue record for this book is available from the British Library.

Printed and bound in Great Britain by Clays Ltd, St Ives plc

DE PARVIS GRANDIS ACERVUS ERIT

*For Xoe, and for Kane and Molly and Fern,
and for Jo and Violet and Quinn and the other Violet and
Ivy, and for Amelia and Lily and Savannah and Jessie and
Megan, and for Sophia and Stella and Flora, and for Mimi
and Beatrix and every brave and clever and curious girl
who lent a word or gesture or look to these characters.
I'm counting on you, kiddos.*

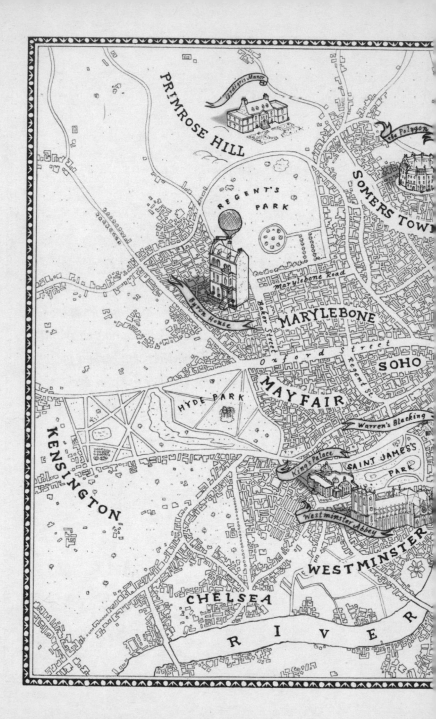

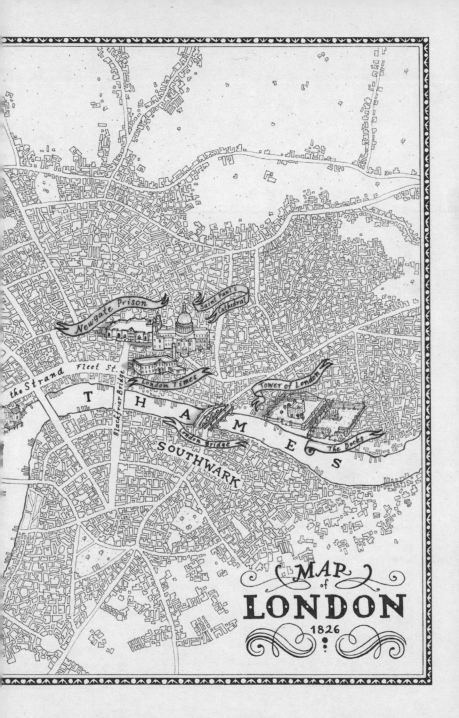

PREFACE

This is a made-up story about two very real girls: Ada Byron, who has been called the world's first computer programmer, and Mary Shelley, the world's first science-fiction author. Ada and Mary didn't really know one another, nor did they have a detective agency together. Mary and Ada were eighteen years apart in age, not three, as they are in the world of Wollstonecraft.

Setting that aside, the characters themselves are as true to history as we are able to tell. At the end of the book, there are notes that reveal more about what happened to each of them in real life, so that you can enjoy the history as much as I hope you'll enjoy the story. Because the history bit is *brilliant*.

— JORDAN STRATFORD

THE
RIDICULOUS HAT

1

"Force . . . equals . . . mass . . . times . . . acceleration," muttered Ada as she wrote in her notebook. Ada pondered that if you drop a hammer on your foot, it hurts more than dropping, say, a sock on your foot. The acceleration, or speeding up, is the same, but the mass, the solid *oomph* of a thing, is different. *Oomph* times *zoom* equals *kaboom*!

Ada and her pondering were cocooned in a square wicker box that resembled a giant picnic basket, just tall enough for her to stand up in and long enough for her to lie down in. Light entered through round, brass-ringed windows and lit up stacks of books, rolls of paper, the odd screwdriver, and a bundle of pencils. The basket hung from thick ropes beneath a vast patchwork balloon that often swayed savagely in the wind, and the whole contraption was tethered with more ropes to the roof of Ada's Marylebone house in the heart of London.

The balloon was one of Ada's best inventions. It was filled with hot air from the house's many chimneys, which Ada funnelled to it via numerous pipes bolted together. Taken as a whole—pipes, ropes, basket and balloon—it gave the impression that the stately house was wearing a sort of ridiculous hat.

Ada lay stretched out on the gondola's floor in her favourite cherry velvet dress, which stopped a full inch above her ankles and showed wear and the odd black grease stain. Her hair was dark brown, almost black, and pulled back into a bun, with little wisps here and there trying to make a run for it.

What if, Ada wondered in her wicker box, you could accelerate a sock? What if the sock were moving so fast that it could have the same force as a hammer? Would it hurt the same? How fast would the sock have to go, and how could you make a sock go that fast?

Ada thought like this all the time. And to capture her thoughts, she made drawings—little sketches in notebooks or on scraps of paper or on table linen or, once (at a very dull picnic and much to the displeasure of her recently former governess, Miss Coverlet), on Ada's new dress. The drawing of the moment was a sock cannon of Ada's invention.

The sock cannon was taking shape on paper and in between Ada's ears. But as busy as her ears were containing the sock-cannon plans, she could make out the sound of a carriage approaching the Marylebone house.

Grabbing a brass telescope that had been rolling about on the floor with the swaying of the basket, she stood and flipped open the hatch. She climbed up the three-step rope ladder to the balloon's short deck, from which she could see as far as Oxford Street. She could see down Wimpole and Welbeck, Wesley and Westmoreland, down Weymouth and Cavendish and Queen Anne and even the little lanes off Baker Street. Only she and the crows knew her neighbourhood in this way, from above.

Her stomach tightened. Walking across busy Marylebone Road, carpetbags in hand, went Miss

Coverlet for the last time, leaving Ada alone for good.

Ada had to admit that "alone" was not entirely accurate. The house in London was staffed by two women whose names she could never quite remember: Misses Cabbage and Cummerbund, or possibly Artichoke and Aubergine—she honestly had no idea. When food arrived—with the exception of the bread and butter she'd help herself to in the upstairs kitchen—it was at the hands of Miss Coverlet, or Ada's very tall and entirely silent butler, Mr Franklin. And then the dishes went away, seemingly by themselves, to a place where she supposed something or other must happen to them.

But as far as Ada was concerned, without Miss Coverlet, whom Ada had known all her life, who had comforted her scrapes and answered her questions and fetched her favourite books and made sure her stockings weren't scratchy—something Ada hated rather desperately—yes, Ada would feel utterly alone.

At eleven, Ada was deemed too old for a governess, and was now to have a tutor instead. A tutor! Ada knew it was impossible for any living person to educate her. For that, she had her books. Books for learning, books for distraction, books for company, books for making sense of things. Ada's books were full of facts and figures, diagrams and calculations. Books that were not to be argued with. Books that stayed put when you needed them to and didn't run off to get married, as Miss Coverlet was off to do, which seemed to Ada like the stupidest idea ever.

In most matters, Ada was a genius. Once the facts and figures and charts and calculations from her books wandered into her head, they never left it. Even when she was a baby, Ada had loved number games and puzzles. She fixed things that were broken, and then began fixing things that weren't broken, or broke things so they could be fixed in ways no one else understood or found particularly convenient. But the one puzzle she couldn't solve was *people*. To Ada, they all seemed to be broken in ways she couldn't make sense of, and couldn't fix.

Right now there was the puzzle of her heart, which was breaking as Miss Coverlet stepped aboard the carriage.

"I'm going to my balloon," Ada had said when informed of Miss Coverlet's departure that morning. She supposed that Miss Coverlet might have mentioned getting married before, but Ada hadn't realized that meant she'd be *leaving* and that *leaving* meant *alone*. And she certainly hadn't known Miss Coverlet would be leaving *today*.

Ada knew that if she was to be alone, then the drawing room, with its grand wallpaper and curlicued gilt frames, its lush Indian carpet and scattering of delicate china, was not where "alone" was going to happen.

Miss Coverlet had watched Ada turn and leave, stomping just a little bit for show. Miss Coverlet had seen some very expert stomping from Ada over the years, and this stomping seemed halfhearted.

Indeed, as Ada now watched Miss Coverlet leave in the carriage, she felt that she had only half a heart left.

Ada had barely returned to her sock-cannon plans when she heard the great black lion's-head knocker strike the front door.

Whoever it was had best go away. She wanted to be left alone—alone as Miss Coverlet had left her, here in her safe wicker fort beneath her balloon, tethered with strong nautical rope to the topmost peak of her house. While she knew she should slide down the rope to the widow's walk and swing into the attic window as she'd done a hundred times before, she felt safest here, basket swaying, with her inventions and her books and her drawings. No, she would not come down.

Not ever.

AWKWARD AND UNCOMFORTABLE

2

Clinging for dear life to a rope atop the Byron house, Percy could not believe that he had missed this from the street. He looked up and contemplated the hot-air balloon with the large, square wicker box attached beneath it. It was a bit windy, and he was not really wearing the right sort of shoes for roof climbing, and certainly not for rope climbing. The whole situation was not only markedly unusual but also awkward and uncomfortable. He decided to call up to the balloon.

"Lady Byron?" Percy called. "Lady Ada?"

"Go away," said a small but determined voice from the wicker box.

"I'm . . . please do allow me to introduce myself. I am Mr . . . er . . . Snagsby, your new tutor."

"Go. Away," said the voice, this time with even more determination.

"I'm to be your new tutor," he shouted over the wind. "I have a letter here from the Baroness Wentworth, um, your mother . . ."

"Are you daft or are you just deaf?" enquired the voice from beneath the hot-air balloon.

"Well, I'm afraid it is a bit windy up here, which can make it a bit difficult to hear exact words, particularly as you're speaking from within what appears to be a gondola of sorts. A gondola is what you call the basket under a hot-air balloon—"

"I *know* what a gondola is. I have one," said the voice.

Percy continued, only slightly deterred, "Well, what I could make out were the words 'go' and 'away'."

"Ah, so not deaf, then."

"No. No, I'm afraid not."

"So just daft, then," deduced the voice.

"I say, that's not terribly fair," huffed Percy.

"Not fair? Not FAIR?" roared the voice from the box. The hatch popped open and Ada's head appeared, her hair even more dishevelled than usual. "I'll tell you what's not fair! It's not *fair* that Miss Coverlet had to go and marry stupid Cecil. It's not *fair* that she's not here and you are! It's not *fair* that my mother has gone to live in the country. It's not *fair* that I can't just be left alone!"

"Lady Ada, if I'm to be your tutor . . ."

"You're not. Go away. There's no one for you to tute."

"I'm quite certain that's not a word," offered Percy.

"Why not? Plumbers plumb. Waiters wait. Butlers buttle. Tutors tute."

"Butlers don't—"

"You're IMPOSSIBLE!" yelled Ada, who disappeared back into the wicker fort and slammed the hatch.

Percy was not, in fact, daft. But he did feel rather daft at that moment, his shoes slipping on the roof tiles as he clung to a knotted rope and stared up at his pupil, who was firmly shut in a large wicker box.

He was startled by the loud clang of a ship's bell

right outside the attic window. He hadn't noticed the bell before, but he certainly had noticed Mr Franklin, the house's extraordinarily tall and curiously silent butler, who now struck the bell once more.

A window popped open on the side of the basket, and the lens of a clicking brass telescope emerged. Ada clearly wanted to see what the bell heralded without having to address Percy. Mr Franklin extended both hands out of the window, one palm up as if to offer something, the other making a winding motion, as though turning a crank.

"It's Mr Babbage!" Ada cried with delight from within the basket. The hatch flew open, and Ada tossed out a rope ladder, scrambled down, and nearly knocked Percy off the roof into the street. Percy slid and clutched desperately at his knotted rope, recovering in time to see a rather worn, stained and outgrown dress clamber over the windowsill and slip into the attic. With no further reason to remain on the roof (although the view was extraordinary), Percy followed, taking it rather personally that clearly not *all* of Lady Ada's visitors were met with such disdain.

Once he was over the windowsill, he fully expected to find himself alone in the attic. It was dusty, as attics ought to be, for mysterious atticky reasons. There were other things one would expect: furniture in ghost costumes of big white sheets, a hobbyhorse long outgrown, large steamer trunks bearing unknown treasures. It also held both Mr Franklin and Ada, who had momentarily suspended her excitement over Mr Babbage's arrival to examine the leather case Percy had left there before heading out onto the roof.

"What's in here?" asked Ada.

"Books," Percy replied.

"What sorts of books?"

"All sorts. History. Language. Poetry . . ."

"I hate poetry," Ada insisted.

"You are not to."

"Not to what?" she asked.

"Not to hate poetry." He was quite emphatic about this point, which got Ada's attention. "But there are other books. Chemistry. Mathematics . . ."

"Mathematics! By whom? What do you have in there?" With that, Ada sat on the floor and began fiddling with the case's brass clasp, finding it locked. "What's this?" she asked, pointing to the small brass plate by the handle. "*PBS*. What's it mean?"

"That's my monogram. My initials. Percy B.—er, Snagsby. It's my name."

"Why'd you do that?"

"Why did I put my monogram on my case? To make it more . . . mine, I suppose."

"Huh," said Ada. It was hard to determine, but it seemed to Percy a rather approving "huh", as far as "huhs" go.

"All right, Peebs. You may show me your books. After."

"Peebs?" asked Percy.

"*PBS*. Peebs. That's your name. Anyway, it shall have to wait until after."

"I'm sorry? After what, Lady Ada?"

"After Mr Babbage, of course! He only comes once a week, so you'll just have to wait." And with a cheerfulness that nearly knocked Percy off his feet, Ada ran to the door and down the stairs.

Percy looked at the looming butler. "Odd," he said. "I was under the impression the young lady was not fond of visitors."

Mr Franklin raised an eyebrow, which silenced Percy completely.

STOWAWAY

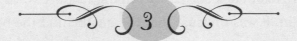

Pitter clop splosh badunk? Clop splosh badunk pitter.

Mary listened to this conversation between the coach, the horse, the cobblestones and the rain, but felt she had little to add. Instead, she observed the unexpected stranger seated opposite her. As far as she could tell, it was a boy of about her age (fourteen), but all she could see of him were knees and feet, clean fingers, and an open book. No matter, she liked him immediately.

Several things were unusual about this carriage ride, and Mary was extremely fond of the unusual.

It smacked of adventure and possibility and mystery, and these things intrigued Mary most of all.

For instance, it was unusual for her to be in a carriage without her sisters or her father. It was also unusual for her to be in a carriage with someone who wasn't any of those people, and unusual indeed for there to be someone already in the carriage when she got in. It was unusual that the boy behind the book had said nothing, but Mary surmised that the boy must be unusually immersed in the book. She decided at once that she and the boy were cut from the same bookish cloth, and could quite possibly become co-conspirators. The thought of this was tremendously exciting, and it inspired Mary to begin a conversation unrelated to the *splosh badunk pitter clop* that was already under way around her.

Mary was most interested in what the boy was reading, which even in the carriage's gloom she could make out was *The History of Tom Jones, a Foundling,* by Henry Fielding, a novel she herself had not read. So instead of *Good morning,* which would have been the expected opening conversational gambit from a young lady of manners when placed in the unusual position of being alone, unchaperoned, in the confined space of a carriage with an unrelated and indeed unfamiliar boy, Mary instead said, "Good book?" which she felt would do quite nicely.

"Mmm," said the boy behind the book.

"I'm afraid I haven't read anything by Fielding. Should I?"

"Mmm-nnn," came the reply, which could have meant *I don't know* or *If you like* or even *Not if you want to be left alone with a book when you're in the unusual position of being alone, unchaperoned, in the confined space of a carriage with an unrelated and indeed unfamiliar girl.*

After an awkward pause, Mary replied with an "Ah." But that seemed to do the trick, so far as breaking the awkward pause went. So she continued.

"This is an unusual position in which to be placed, isn't it? Sharing the carriage, I mean."

"Not to be rude," replied the boy. "But it would be greatly appreciated if you could pretend that I'm not here. I'm not supposed to be."

"Whyever not?" asked Mary.

"I haven't money for a carriage. So I'm not supposed to be here. Also, it's the only time today I'll be able to read."

"Good heavens!" exclaimed Mary in hushed, conspiratorial tones. "Are you a stowaway?"

"No, no. It's nothing like that. It's an exchange. I trade with the coachman. I help him, and he lets me read in the mornings in the carriage, so long as I pretend I'm not here and nobody minds."

"Oh, I see. And how do you help him?" Mary found this new world of secrets and stowaways terribly adventurous. *Romantic,* even, though not in a smoochy way.

"He gets letters. From his mum. And he likes to send word back. So I read and write his letters for him."

"The coachman is unable to read or write?"

"He never went to school, and nobody taught him. It's not his fault."

"No, of course not. It's very kind of you to help him."

"It's very kind of *him* to drive me to work in the rain and give me a moment to read."

"Well, yes, I suppose it is," admitted Mary.

The boy put the book down, revealing that there was a perfectly normal boy behind it. She had begun to harbour a sneaking suspicion—and Mary was inordinately fond of sneaking suspicions—that he might be hideously disfigured, or possibly a very famous young prince or duke in hiding, afraid to show his face. But he was neither hideous nor recognizably famous. Just a boy, with a book.

"You won't tell, will you?" he asked.

"I'm terribly good at keeping secrets," Mary assured him.

The boy squeezed out a small smile and returned behind *The History of Tom Jones, a Foundling,* by Henry Fielding. Unfortunately, this created for Mary another awkward pause.

"Mary Godwin," she said, holding out her hand.

"Charles," said the boy, who stuck out his hand without putting the book down. This left Mary the task of coordinating the handshake in the gloom of the carriage.

"I'm very pleased to meet you, Charles. My baby brother bears the same name."

"Mmm," Charles replied, having descended once more into his story.

Pitter clop clop badunk splosh whoa! said the horse, and the road, and the rain, and the coachman, indicating that this was Mary's destination.

"Enjoy your day, and I do hope I'll see you to-morrow."

Mary departed the carriage without waiting for an additional "Mmm" from her new friend, stepping into Marylebone Road.

In that half a heartbeat between descending from the carriage and touching down onto the cobblestones, Mary struggled to remember the name of a butterfly. She knew it was the largest in the world, the width of both her hands splayed out, and that it had deep brown eyes painted on soft pink velvet wings. She knew too, from her reading, that it was only found in the remotest jungles of Papua New Guinea in the South Pacific Ocean, half the world away. She was surprised, therefore, to discover that such a thing was flying between her stomach and her heart, its wings brushing against her ribs and pushing the air out of her with each beat.

Riding in a carriage unchaperoned was a brave and arguably rebellious act for a fourteen-year-old girl. Discovering a stowaway was another sort of adventure altogether. But arriving at the house of the great, mad, dead poet Lord Byron, to be tutored alongside an actual Lady, was almost too much to bear. Or so the giant butterfly whispered to her stomach.

But this was not a storybook adventure like the ones Mary read and reread by lantern light until the dim of each night overtook her. This was a real adventure, with herself in a starring role. It was this, or the dreaded, confining, dull grey horror of "school", about which Mary had only heard from cousins. Still, in that half a heartbeat, Mary put down the need to name the butterfly and blew it out of her chest like puffing out a candle. The toe of her shoe touched the earth, and her adventure would be what it would be.

INCENDIARY

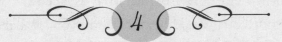

Mary stepped into the London rain. It had been a brief carriage ride, perhaps only ten minutes, from the Godwin house in Somers Town to her destination in Marylebone.

On the doorstep of the Byron house, Mary saw a gaunt fellow of unnatural height standing under the small porch roof and holding the door open. He kept vigil over a sight that was, for Mary, even more unusual than her encounter with the secret boy in the carriage.

Mary watched as a girl, perhaps eleven, rain-soaked

in a once-pretty but now filthy and outgrown gown, poked at a heap of horse dung with a short-handled coal shovel.

Determined to make a good first impression, Mary had prepared a clear-throated *Good morning,* a handshake or curtsy as circumstances may dictate, and a self-introduction. Instead, what escaped her was a less courteous "Good heavens! What on *earth* are you doing?"

"Potassium nitrate," Ada replied.

"Ah," said Mary, not sure what that was or if it might explain anything.

"I read that the ancient Chinese used horse dung as a source of potassium nitrate crystals. But no joy here," Ada said, disgruntled. "Just soggy horse poo."

"So it would seem," said Mary. "If I may, had you found some . . ." Mary had to think for a minute.

"Potassium nitrate."

"Right. Well, what would you use it for?"

"I'd add it to the charcoal."

"The charcoal," Mary repeated.

"Willow. Brilliant stuff. Long as you keep the oxygen down while it burns, crisps up good as anything."

"So, the horse dung combines with the charcoal?"

"Yes. After that, sulphur. Have to send Mr Franklin to the chemist for that, I expect."

Mary assumed that Mr Franklin must be the very tall butler on the doorstep, and noticed that Ada hadn't seemed to notice that this conversation was taking place in the street, in the rain, without introduction. Which struck Mary as unusual and, therefore, interesting. She persevered.

"So dung and charcoal and sulphur make . . . ?"

"Gunpowder," explained Ada. "Or it's supposed to. Haven't tried it before. I think this poo is too wet."

"Gunpowder," acknowledged Mary. "That does sound a little . . . incendiary." Then, remembering the age of the girl with the shovel, she added, "'Incendiary' means—"

"Explosive. Making fire. Kaboom."

"Quite." Clearly, the younger girl needed no assistance so far as vocabulary was concerned.

"Nothing incendiary here. Just poo."

"That is unfortunate," replied Mary. "Would you mind terribly if I asked what the gunpowder is for?"

Ada frowned deeply. She darted the coal shovel into the dung, where it stood for only a brief moment and then fell sadly to the pavement with a skitter and clang.

"It was," said Ada, "for my sock cannon. Only, I've been making it bigger so it can be a Peebs cannon."

"How extraordinary. And what, pray tell, is a Peebs cannon?"

"A cannon. For shooting Peebs out of."

Baffled still, Mary tried a new tack. "I don't wish to be a bother, but would you mind terribly if I came in? It's raining."

"Is it?" Ada looked up, squinted, and looked down at her dress, which was even more soaked than Mary's. "Best come in, then." At this, Ada turned and marched into the house, past the very tall man, who stood and waited for Mary. She gave at last the curtsy she had prepared, but as this resulted largely in a shower of drips upon the man's shoes, it wasn't quite the impression she'd hoped for.

The house, however, made quite an impression on Mary. It was almost impossibly grand compared to the homey-messy-busy Godwin house, which overflowed with sisters and the baby and toys and books. The Byron house was a thing of gleaming marble and white banisters. A house for a Lady. *A baroness,* Mary reminded herself. Oddly, the Byron house seemed almost empty, and surprisingly clean. Given the drips and soot and mud in Ada's wake, Mary assumed it must be quite the job to keep it this way.

"Lady Ada!" came a man's voice from up the stairs. "Lady Ada!"

Mary couldn't help noticing that Ada walked away down the hall, as though she'd heard nothing.

Footsteps hurriedly descended the white stairs, bringing with them a tallish, slenderish, reddish-haired young man, book in hand, shirtsleeves rolled up to his elbows. He paused when he saw that it was Mary and not Ada at the bottom.

"Ah! You must be Miss Godwin," the young man pronounced. "So delighted, I'm sure. I'm Mr Shell—er, Snagsby—"

"He's Peebs!" shouted Ada from down the hall.

The man grimaced. "Well, yes, I suppose I am Peebs. In this house, at least."

Mary smiled and curtsied again, a little more dignified this time.

"Mary Godwin, Mr Peebs, and very pleased to meet you."

"He's not *Mr Peebs*," mumbled Ada through a mouthful of bread and butter as she returned to the front hall. "Just Peebs."

"Very well, then," said Mary. "Just Peebs." And after a moment for her brain to catch up, she added an "Oh!" when she realized that the gunpowder—dung, charcoal, sulphur and all—was in aid of launching this poor fellow out of a cannon. Probably against his wishes and better judgement.

Ada merely cocked an eyebrow.

"Notwithstanding," said Peebs, which made Ada think of sitting, "we shall commence our studies in the drawing room. If you'd like to follow me."

Mary would very much have liked to follow him, but Ada said "Don't" in a very decisive voice.

"Don't?"

"You'll only encourage him."

Mary collected herself, the unusual circumstances of the introduction making the task slightly easier, and gave a deep, neat curtsy.

"Lady Ada, I'm very pleased to make your acquaintance. I'm Mary, Mary Godwin. And I'm to be tutored alongside you, under . . . um . . . Peebs."

Ada looked suddenly cross. "You can't be serious. I don't know you."

"I should very much like you to," said Mary, the giant butterfly stirring in her chest once again. The opportunity to be tutored with Ada had been hastily and somewhat mysteriously arranged by her family's patron, and she wanted quite desperately to show herself worthy of it. It seemed unwise to reveal so much so soon, so Mary contented herself with "I have the surest feeling we are to be the best of friends."

"He's entirely useless," said Ada rudely, with Peebs standing right there.

"Steady on," interjected Peebs.

"It's true. He can barely seem to remember his own name, and he doesn't know anything worth knowing. Just Greek, and poetry."

"I adore poetry," Mary said, feeling bad for Peebs standing there and being insulted.

"Ugh," said Ada definitively.

"But Greek!" tried Peebs. "The language of the philosophers. And of science! Plato, and Archimedes . . ."

"*Eureka,*" admitted Ada, although Mary had no idea what she meant by it.

"Miss Godwin," said Peebs, enjoying the rare and momentary victory, "I seem to have failed to introduce myself to your chaperone."

"I arrived unchaperoned," said Mary proudly. She thought briefly of Charles, and wondered if he counted as a "chaperone" but decided that he did not, seeing as he wasn't officially there. "Our family is quite modern."

"I imagine so, Miss Godwin," said Peebs. "I was greatly impressed by your mother's work."

All this seemed far too conspiratorial for Ada's liking. Why was this new girl in her house? Who arranged it? How did Peebs know of Mary's mother's work? And what was it?

Too much, is what it was. Ada didn't know why, but she felt like either crying or breaking things. She found herself pulling at the fabric of her dress, something Miss Coverlet constantly chided her for doing. And this made her more upset—both because she was doing something without meaning to and because Miss Coverlet was no longer there to chide her for it.

Ada fled up the stairs, and not to the drawing room to study Greek.

LAVENDER

5

The next two weeks for Mary progressed along simi-
lar lines: riding unchaperoned with the reading boy
who pretended he wasn't there, stepping past the
mysteriously silent butler (could he speak? dare he
not? was he the bearer of some grim secret?), settling
down to study in the drawing room, and marvelling
at Ada's refusal to do the same.

Mary dutifully attended to her studies, and found
Peebs personable and instructive. Occasionally, Ada
would be in the drawing room, although she gave the
impression of having found herself there by accident,

nose in a book. She never took the slightest notice of Peebs. Often she would rise while he was in mid-sentence and simply wander off like a sleepwalker, still reading, in her increasingly filthy dress.

Ada's dress, perhaps originally of a cherry velvet, had blotched and frayed and snagged to the point where it seemed like a circus tent after one too many seasons in the rain. The dress had become, to Mary, as much a fixture of the house as the imposing Mr Franklin, the marble of the foyer, and the rooftop balloon. To satisfy her curiosity, Peebs had taken Mary to the attic, where she had leaned out of the window to marvel at the tangled maze of pipes and ropes that kept Ada's balloon aloft and tethered. Indeed, she was quite keen to venture out and up to the balloon itself, but didn't want to intrude on Ada, who had raised the rope ladder behind her.

One morning, when Ada failed to appear entirely, Peebs indicated to Mary that the young Lady Byron had locked herself in her room, which was unlike her. Ada had a variety of locations into which she liked to lock herself, and her bedroom wasn't usually one of them. Mary decided to investigate.

She rapped upon the stout white door.

"Go away," came Ada's voice from the other side.

Over the previous fortnight, Mary had heard several variations of Ada's "Go away," and knew they could mean different things. But this was the first time Mary had had one delivered to her directly.

"Ada, it's me, Mary."

"Go away."

"What's wrong? I can probably help."

"Can't," declared Ada.

Mary took a moment, steeled herself, and spoke firmly to the door.

"Can."

There was a good moment of silence, and then the key turned in the lock on the inside, which was all the invitation Mary was likely to get.

Mary entered Ada's bedroom for the first time. The word "disaster" presented itself to Mary. It does a good job of describing things like earthquakes and mudslides and tornadoes, but it was simply not up to the task of describing Ada's bedroom. Mary suddenly felt sorry for the word.

There were books, of course, in sliding piles, propped open and dog-eared. An oilcan was upended and seeping black into the carpet, and several inkpots had done the same. Poking halfway out from beneath the bed was a great iron wrench the size of Mary's arm. There were odd and chunky bits of brass, like one might find on a ship, and drawings pinned to the wall in clumps as though they'd grown there. There were dolls, but only in parts, and frequently combined with spring-wound contraptions, abandoned midconstruction.

Ada, in her nightdress, had sat back down on the only clear spot of bed, hot tears streaking her face.

"Oh dear, Ada," said Mary. "What on earth has happened?" She might have been discussing the state of Ada's bedroom, but all that concerned her was Ada's tears.

"She washed it."

"Who washed it? What it?" Mary wanted to correct her own grammar, but she found it too easy to slip into Ada's little bursts of information. Mary had learned Ada had two distinct ways of speaking: her usual steady flow of facts and observations and conversation and the odd, choppy, disconnected word scraps that came out when she was frustrated or merely distracted.

"My dress. She washed it. Wrong."

Indeed, there was Ada's once-cherry dress wadded up into a bundle on the bed. The word "washed" might have been overreaching; "defilthed" would be more accurate.

"It looks quite serviceable to me. I'm sure it's perfectly fine."

"Smells wrong."

Mary took the velvet bundle and gave it an investigative sniff.

"Lavender."

"Not supposed to."

"Dear Ada, I can hardly follow you at all when you're like this. Not supposed to what?"

"Smell. Like lavender. Like anything," said Ada, her words choppy between sobs.

"Well," suggested Mary calmly, "we might ask Anna to wash it again, only without lavender."

Ada suddenly seemed un-upset. In fact, there wasn't even the customary sniff or tear-wipe one might expect when someone who was recently crying isn't any more. It was like a switch being thrown. There was crying-Ada, and then there wasn't.

"Who's Anna?" Ada asked, without a touch of emotion.

"Anna. Miss Cumberland. She's the maid."

"Whose maid?"

"*Your* maid. She lives here, in the house."

"Does she?" Ada seemed to recall something about that, a Miss Cucumber, or Cabinet, from downstairs.

"Yes. She'd like to be a lady's maid someday, but for now she's the housemaid."

"I didn't know there were different kinds," said Ada, wondering why she didn't know that. "How do you know about her?"

"I asked," said Mary.

Ada found that comforting, asking and finding out. "What's your mother's work?" asked Ada, changing the subject.

"Pardon?" Mary found herself confused by Ada's rapid change of mood and subjects.

"Peebs said something about your mother's work. What does she do?"

"She wrote. She was a writer. She said that men and women should only be as different as they wish to be, and that education and profession should be available to all."

"Well, that makes sense," said Ada. It seemed

rather obvious to be considered a "work", though, in her estimation.

"She died when I was very small," added Mary. "I don't remember her."

Ada was suddenly uncomfortable with the small sadness in Mary's words.

"My father was a writer too," Ada blurted. "He's dead as well. When I was eight."

"I'm very sorry," said Mary.

"I didn't really know him. And Mother won't talk about him. She won't let his books in the house. His friends used to come to visit, but she shooed them away."

"May I ask how your father died?" said Mary cautiously.

"Three years ago, in Greece. There was a war. I've seen all the maps. He went to fight for the Greeks so they could have their own country. And he got sick and died."

"Oh dear. But that's very brave. An extraordinary adventure."

Ada had heard this before, about her father, but such comments always evoked her mother's displeasure. She wasn't sure what to think.

"How did your mother die?" asked Ada.

"Making me," said Mary.

"I'm glad," said Ada, and immediately realized it was a horrible thing to say. She wasn't glad that Mary's mother died. She was just glad that Mary got made, that's all she meant. She suddenly felt very stupid, and angry at herself.

Mary noticed that Ada was holding her breath.

Mary too had been shocked by Ada's words, but quickly saw that Ada was unused to talking about feelings, hers or anyone else's, and had meant no harm. Mary could see it in her eyes, along with a sheen of embarrassment.

"Thank you," said Mary, clearly understanding what was meant.

Ada exhaled.

"Now," added Mary, "let's see Anna about that dress, shall we?"

THE BLEH

The following week was one of fast friendship for Ada and Mary, and Mary was let in on three secrets.

The first, to Mary's delight, was the balloon. Mary found that even though she was a forehead taller than Ada, she could stand in her stocking feet inside the room-that-was-a-wicker-basket and just barely fit. She'd suggested bringing up a little table and chairs so that the two of them could take their tea in the gondola, and Ada seemed pleased at the idea.

The second secret was in the form of a visitor, a Mr Babbage. Ada came to life whenever she spoke of him or of her anticipation of his visits. One day, when Ada had disappeared from the drawing room, where their studies had been laid out, Mary went to see where Ada had wandered off to, which was the library, as it was more often than not.

Mary found Ada seated on the floor, but curiously enough she was neither reading nor drawing. She was merely sitting, her back tall and straight and her legs tied up in some sort of knot. While this struck Mary as remarkable, it was less remarkable than the sight of a grown gentleman, slightly portly and balding but well attired, seated likewise on the floor opposite Ada with his eyes closed.

"This is Mr Babbage," whispered Ada without moving. "Don't speak to him."

"All right," agreed Mary in hushed tones. "What is happening, exactly?"

Ada remained motionless and breathed slowly before answering.

"Mr Babbage's friend Mr Everest has returned from India with some interesting ideas about mathematics. We're to sit like this and imagine ourselves as points on a curve, and then write equations about it."

"Are you really?" said Mary, simply because she couldn't think of anything else to say. None of this looked like her idea of mathematical equations at all. It looked like sitting on the floor.

"Mr Babbage says this is how you imagine things in India. Mr Everest showed him."

Still not knowing what to say, and not meaning to intrude, Mary excused herself politely and left Ada to her silent friend.

Ada's third secret—which she didn't keep on purpose, she just had no one to mention it to—was "the bleh", or at least that's what Ada called it. The Byron Lignotractatic Engine, or BLE. And it was marvellous in the way that such perfect, intricate things are marvellous. It lived in a darkened room off the library, a panelled, forgotten room that may, in the long history of the house, have been intended for storage, as it had no windows to the outside world.

The bleh reminded Mary of the workings of a music box—spools of sprockets with tiny hammers that did or didn't click on a bumpy bit. But the bleh was a chorus of music boxes, a symphony of them, and its music, Ada explained, was numbers. You set the tiny spools in rows to represent numbers, wound up the engine in different ways depending on what you wanted to do with them, adding or subtracting or multiplying or dividing and remembering, and let it clack away on springs and ratchets so that different numbers finally emerged.

"What kind of numbers?" Mary enquired.

"Anything can be numbers," said Ada. "That's the trick. Here, look." And she released the winding spring so that all the spindles spun in their slots, then settled with a satisfying click, as if to announce something.

Mary was still puzzled.

"Not down here, look up there." Ada pointed to a row of upright brass rods, some thirty-two of them, each with a stack of wooden cubes strung down it. Mary could see that each side of each cube was stained a slightly different shade of brown, from light to dark. The rods had gears along the bottom, and all of that was connected to the cabinet of spindles beneath.

"Watch," said Ada.

Mary stepped back as Ada once again ran the engine, clicking along its conversation of numbers. But this time, Mary's attention was on the towers of little

blocks strung along the brass rods. It took her a moment to understand what she was seeing.

A horse. Galloping.

Each cube, now light, now dark, fluttered in place, and the blocks together made a picture, and that picture was *moving*. Alive. Wondrous. A horse galloping along a forest of wooden cubes, over and over and over.

Mary didn't realize that her hand was over her mouth until she saw Ada's eyebrow at that odd angle again. Mary laughed at herself.

"When you say anything can be numbers," asked Mary, "what do you mean?"

"This horse. Maps. Leaves. Things that move."

"People?"

"People, I suppose. I'm . . . better at some numbers than others."

"This is marvellous," said Mary.

"I know. That's what Mr Babbage has been helping me with. Or me him. The numbers. You need numbers to turn things into other numbers."

"It's magic."

"No, it's simple. There's just a simple thing, and another simple thing, and another, and another, piled on top of each other. The whole is big, but each thing is simple. You just need to keep track."

"Like a pianoforte," Mary offered.

"I don't know how to play the piano," said Ada, wondering for the first time if she should.

"Each key pushes a hammer," Mary explained. "The hammer hits a string inside the piano and plays one note. Just one. But play the keys together and you get music."

"The bleh," said Ada, smiling with delight, holding out her hand in a now-you-finally-get-it gesture.

"More," said Mary breathlessly. "Show me more."

And Ada did, and Mary marvelled, until the carriage arrived to take her home to the Godwin house in Somers Town.

THE VERY.
GOOD. IDEA.

7

With increasing frequency, Ada took to sitting along-side Mary while Peebs tutored. She didn't really participate, although she did offer the occasional correction when Peebs got something wrong.

When Ada did engage Peebs, it was usually to ask if he had a book on a particular subject. If he did not, he'd bring one the next morning, and she'd spend the day engrossed.

Few things distracted Ada from her bubble of reading. But she did note a curious exchange between Mary and Peebs, and a second curious exchange between Peebs and Mary. Ada had never been ter-ribly good at picking up on curious exchanges, and was pleased to think she was getting better at it.

In the first exchange, Ada could tell that Mary was unusually emotional about thanking Peebs for being her tutor. It turned out, as Ada listened intently, that Mary's only alternative would have been to be sent away to school. This thought visibly frightened Mary— being away from her family, enduring a school's strict order and endless recitation, and being struck with a cane for breaking rules you might not even know about. This was all awful, of course, but what inter-ested Ada most were little nuances she'd never noticed before: a certain something in Mary's voice, the way the pupils of her eyes got bigger, how her mouth tight-ened ever so slightly. All these things were being cata-logued and labelled and filed away in Ada's brain for later reference. *So this is what happens when people are upset and trying not to show how much,* she thought. *Fascinating.*

The second exchange—and this was quite bril-liant as far as Ada was concerned—occurred when Peebs showed up late and out of sorts and confessed to Mary that he had been particularly distressed by a story in the newspaper about impoverished orphans.

Ada noted that as he talked, bright red spots appeared on his cheeks, which was interesting, but the brilliant part was the newspaper itself.

Ada had never given much thought to newspapers before, but as soon as she looked at one, it was like opening a hundred books at once. Odd, disconnected bits of information. Names. Deaths and marriages. Fires and kidnappings. Courts and magistrates. Announcements of inventions and medicines. Information that might take years to find its way into books.

Some of this was clearly rubbish—one bit would contradict the bit right next to it, and they couldn't both be true, which led Ada to wonder who was putting this newspaper together in the first place. What frustrated Ada was that as soon as she became interested in a bit of information in the newspaper, the article was over. When she expressed this, Peebs told her there would be another newspaper the next day with more information, and Ada could scarcely believe she'd been missing out on this small miracle all this time.

Days passed in a new routine of Ada's descending the stairs upon Mary's arrival, and of Peebs's gifting of the morning's paper. Ada would spend much of the morning reading, interrupting Peebs to ask him the odd question to determine if the scandals of members of Parliament might be interesting (they weren't), and then more or less settling into a comfortable fog of carpets and tea and tinkering and drawing and biscuits.

"Crime," said Ada one afternoon, out of nowhere, while reading the newspaper. There was a goodly bit about crime in the newspaper.

"Mmm?" Mary had been reading too, a book on Greek mythology. Orpheus was climbing the long stair out of the underworld and was about to take a forbidden glance at Eurydice to see if she was still there. Mary always wanted to shout at him not to do it.

"Crime," Ada repeated. "I've never really thought about it before."

"I imagine there's much wickedness in the world," answered Mary, detached.

"Why?" asked Ada.

"I cannot say. Perhaps it is just in our nature," said Mary, looking up from her book.

"But you have a nature, and you're not a criminal." And after a pause, Ada added, "Are you?"

"Heavens, no. One makes choices. Choices have

consequences," Mary repeated, although she couldn't say from where.

"So, criminals are choosing to be criminals." Ada had a way of asking questions that didn't sound like questions, and Mary had a way of knowing when.

"I suppose so. I think it depends on the crime. If you're starving and steal bread, I imagine you don't have much of a choice. But if you're a kidnapper, or a highwayman, then, yes, these are choices. I've never really thought about it."

"Criminals aren't very clever," Ada declared.

"No?"

"No. They get caught. It's always in the newspaper. Only they don't say 'caught', they say 'apprehended', which means the same thing."

"Well, I imagine 'Criminal Not Getting Apprehended' wouldn't make much of a newspaper story, so they probably leave that bit out."

"Leave bits out? Of the newspaper?"

"Well, I'm only supposing. But I can hardly see them putting things in the newspaper that *don't* happen."

"No," agreed Ada. "That makes sense." She pondered. "So the newspaper criminals are the not-clever ones, and the ones that aren't in the newspaper must be clever."

"Not as clever as you, I'm sure," said Mary.

"Probably not," admitted Ada. She wasn't boasting; it was just very likely to be true.

"I imagine," said Mary, her mind returning to her book, "that you could apprehend quite a few criminals. Being more clever than them."

"That would at least put them in the newspaper," agreed Ada, the idea striking her as rather tidy somehow. Once things were in the newspaper, they were almost as good as being in books, and that meant she had a place in her brain to put them. Like solving a puzzle. "I could be a magistrate, or on the constabulary, and put criminals in the newspaper."

"Prison," corrected Mary. "Criminals go to prison, not to the newspaper." This point seemed completely irrelevant to Ada. "But you couldn't, of course. Young ladies cannot be magistrates, or on the constabulary."

"Why not?" asked Ada.

"Because we are young ladies. And you especially are a young Lady. Big *L*. It's simply not allowed."

Ada was displeased at this. "Your mum wrote that book," she said.

Mary was puzzled, thinking Ada was referring to the half-closed Greek mythology book Mary page-kept with her thumb.

"Your mum wrote that girls can do whatever," Ada continued. "Education. Profession."

Mary, now fully engaged, put down her book.

"My dear Ada, my mother wrote about how things ought to be, not how they are."

Ada continued looking displeased, which made Mary go on. "Of course, how are things to be the way they ought, unless we make them so? And if clever criminals can make choices to become criminal and remain clever enough to not go to prison—or the newspaper," she added for Ada's benefit, "then why *can't* we be magistrates or on the constabulary? In fact, we ought to be, if we so choose."

"Well, we can't," said Ada. "I'm only eleven. And you're fourteen."

"There is that," admitted Mary.

"And if Mother or Peebs found out, they would be . . ."

"Yes?"

"Incendiary," said Ada.

"Theoretically, that would only be if they found out," said Mary cautiously.

"A secret constabulary, then," said Ada. Thus satisfied, she returned to her newspaper.

To Mary's way of thinking, rather a lot depended on words. And to her, the word "secret" meant intrigue. Adventure. Romance. It meant everything that Mary, in her fourteen-year-old heart of hearts, knew that she *was*. The word "secret" had suddenly made Mary's heart bang around madly in her ribs, as the butterfly had done weeks before. She thought she was going to burst.

"This," said Mary as calmly as she could, which was hardly at all, "is a very. Good. Idea."

"What is?" said the part of Ada that wasn't reading the newspaper, having forgotten already.

"A secret constabulary," replied Mary. "Except they are called 'private detectives'. A detective agency." And she leaned forward for full effect, whispering, "A secret one."

Ada still wasn't fully aware of what Mary was saying, and continued with the part of her brain that didn't think it needed to be.

"You could put an advertisement in the news-paper," she suggested, without enthusiasm.

"How can we advertise something that's secret?" asked Mary.

"Well," said Ada, a bit more of her brain paying attention, "you could say there's a detective agency and keep secret the bit where it's us."

"You know, that's terribly clever."

"Mmm," agreed Ada.

"We'll need to come up with a secret name. Or rather, a name for the secret. To put in the advertise-ment. In the newspaper."

"You should call it after your mum; it was her idea," said Ada, which it wasn't, not technically, but Mary knew what she meant. "What was her name?"

"Mary," said Mary.

"That's not a very good secret name. It's yours. Did she have another name?"

"Wollstonecraft," said Mary, smiling. And that was that.

THE
ADVERTISEMENT

8

That, as it turned out, was not entirely that. While the girls, who had increasingly begun to think of themselves as the Wollstonecraft girls, made plans and imagined the adventures that were sure to come, there was still the matter of the advertisement. And Peebs.

Mr Franklin, Ada assured Mary, could be trusted to occupy or divert Peebs as needed. Mary wasn't exactly sure how this was supposed to happen, but Ada was quite confident in the matter. Mr Franklin had been in Ada's life since she was a baby, and she trusted him like no one else.

As for the advertisement itself, deciding on what it was to say was the easy part. Mary wrote, and Ada agreed to:

WOLLSTONECRAFT DETECTIVE AGENCY
A PRIVATE & SECRET CONSTABULARY
FOR THE APPREHENSION OF
CLEVER CRIMINALS

Beneath this was a request to forward enquiries to the *Times* office itself, where, Mary assured Ada, there were slots for accepting whatever letters they might receive in response. The girls would some-how have to ensure that these letters were collected daily.

Getting the advertisement to the newspaper, however, would have to be, as Mary pointed out, clandestine. She opened her mouth to explain that "clandestine" was another word for "secret", but then imagined Ada rolling her eyes and insisting that she knew already, so Mary closed her mouth again.

"Why clandestine?" asked Ada.

"Dear Ada, a girl can hardly appear at *The Times* on her own, on such extraordinary business."

"You could be running an errand for someone else."

"That would be unlikely, as no one would send a girl on such an errand. On any errand, really, except perhaps an errand between other young ladies. Which would omit *The Times*."

"You come here on your own," Ada pointed out. "Or at least you intend to."

"Riding in a carriage without an escort is modern. But travelling out and about unescorted is unheard of."

"Why?"

"Ada! A young lady needs to protect her reputation. I can't imagine what it would do to my family for someone to even think that something improper was going on where I was concerned."

"What's improper about placing an advertisement in the newspaper?"

"Nothing, except of course when one wishes to keep such matters in confidence. But it's the appearance of the thing. They'd throw me out on the street were I to show up on my own."

"They wouldn't dare!" said Ada, shocked.

"They would, Ada. They would."

"That's not fair!"

"No, it isn't. But it's the way it is. So we need a plan."

It took a full day for Mary to figure it out, but she finally realized that she already knew someone who was very good at being clandestine.

The next morning when the carriage came by the Godwin house, Mary was prepared.

"Charles?" she said to the boy behind *Ivanhoe,* by Sir Walter Scott.

"I'm not supposed to be here," said Charles.

"We've been through that. Yes, you're not here. Understood. And that makes you perfectly suited for the task circumstance compels me to bestow upon you."

"Are you," said Charles after a moment, "a damsel in distress?"

Mary thought about that. "Not really, no."

"There are damsels in distress in *Ivanhoe,*" Charles stated.

Mary persevered. "But I am a friend in need. And rather specifically, in need of your not being here. Officially, that is to say."

"You need me to leave?"

"No, no. Well, yes, actually. What I mean to say is—you said you worked?"

"Mmm," came the reply, Charles being clearly uninterested in the subject.

"What do you do, if you don't mind terribly my asking?"

"I work at the boot-polish factory. I glue the labels on."

"That must be . . . very . . ." said Mary, "um . . ."

"It is," said Charles.

"But you can get to places. Unchaperoned. Places like *The Times*."

"You want me to travel in time?"

"*Times. The*. The newspaper. I require someone"— and for the second time that week, she leaned forward to whisper loudly for emphasis—"clandestine."

"Then, fair maiden, I shall be your gallant," said Charles, suddenly fully present. She assumed his answer must be something from his book.

"Brilliant!" said Mary, her enthusiasm overtaking her. "I'd be ever so grateful if you would place this advertisement in the newspaper and, of course, retrieve the replies, should there be any, in the coming days.

Here's tuppence for the ad. And here"—she handed him a slip of paper—"is what we need it to say. Only please, keep it clandestine."

Charles had put his book away altogether. "You have my word, m'lady." With this, he half stood, placed his hand across his heart with a half-bow, opened the door, and leaped out of the carriage.

Alone, unchaperoned and un-Charlesed, Mary wondered for the first time about the consequences of her choices.

MISSIVES

A pattern emerged. Mary began each day scrambling for the basin and clothes and breakfast amid the door-banging of her sisters, Fanny and Jane, and the wailing of baby Charles. As Mary entered the coach each morning, the not-her-baby-brother Charles would hand her a bundle of envelopes he'd picked up from the Wollstonecraft slot at *The Times*. Each envelope would contain a case, or a question, or in some cases just nonsense that people would send for reasons Mary could not imagine. The envelope bundle would remain, unopened, in Mary's schoolbag throughout the morning's tutorial session while Mary listened attentively to Peebs, and Ada read the newspaper.

At noon, the girls would retire to the balloon, where Mary would read the contents of the envelopes aloud. Ada would lean back in a small wicker chair, almost to the tipping point, and listen with eyes closed.

"No," said Ada, at the conclusion of each reading.

Mary had stopped asking why after the first dozen, and had ceased becoming frustrated after the second. Some of Ada's nos were obvious—some cases were too broad or too far. There were just the two of them, and they had to remain fairly close to the Marylebone house. And several cases seemed unpleasant in a way that didn't feel all that adventurous. But others, Mary was sure, would appeal to Ada, or at least to Ada's desire to put clever criminals in the newspaper. So far, she had been wrong.

"No," said Ada once again, at the completion of another letter. There was only one more in today's bundle, and Mary opened it with a resigned pull of the letter opener.

"All right, this one is from a Miss Rebecca Verdigris . . ."

"Aha!" exclaimed Ada, without opening her eyes.

"What? I haven't read it yet."

"Name, in the newspaper. Go on."

"All right. She says, 'Dear Wollstonecraft Detectives,' some pleasantries, and here we go: 'dire need of assistance . . . precious object stolen . . . constables have apprehended my maid, who has confessed, although I am certain of her innocence . . .'"

"Honestly?" asked Ada. "They've already apprehended the thief?"

"Well, they've apprehended someone, but Miss Verdigris here insists they've got the entirely wrong someone."

"That's interesting."

"I'm sure it's awful," said Mary.

"But it would take a *clever* criminal to put the constables on to the *wrong* criminal. So that's a yes, then."

"Are you—"

"Yes."

"And you're quite—"

"Certainly."

"What about—"

"This one." Ada was determined.

"Right, then," said Mary. "I'll ask Charles to deliver a message to Miss Verdigris in the morning."

"Today. Ask Mathilda to do it."

"Mathilda?" asked Mary, confused.

"Your friend. The one who lives downstairs."

"Anna? Your maid?"

"That's the one."

"Well! Today, then. We'll draft a note for Anna and send for a carriage."

Ada rose suddenly, flipping open the side hatch and letting in a blast of cool air.

"She won't need one," said Ada, pointing north over the rooftops of Baker Street to the rising green slope of Regent's Park and Primrose Hill. "Our case is right there."

REBECCA

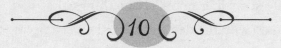

Things had progressed rather quickly that afternoon. Ada had dictated a note in reply to Miss Verdigris's request for help, which Mary softened and sprinkled with appropriate courtesies. Anna had been dispatched with the message, and this mission pleased her tremendously, as it was the sort of thing done by a lady's maid, which she wanted to be, and not a housemaid, which she was.

Anna, of course, knew nothing of the secret nature of the message, and it seemed to her perfectly ordinary for one young lady to ask another to come and visit, even though this had never happened before.

The only issue that remained was what was to be done with Peebs.

He had been picking scraps of paper off the drawing-room floor—Ada had developed a habit of hastily scrawling notes about things that had nothing to do with the day's studies, then crumpling them and tossing them at him absentmindedly—when he saw the imposing figure of Mr Franklin looming in the doorway.

It wasn't so much that Mr Franklin made Peebs nervous as it was that his appearance made him feel that a vast bronze statue had suddenly sprung up without explanation in odd places about the house— the bottom of the stairs or the middle of the hallway. Just something large and solid that had to be dealt with or at the very least walked round.

Mr Franklin did not, or possibly could not, speak, but he made himself perfectly clear through a variety of subtle expressions. The one he offered Peebs (by raising his left eyebrow ever so slightly) seemed to say *Come with me or I may step on you by accident and it is not likely you would enjoy the experience.*

So when he turned and walked downstairs, Peebs followed dutifully.

Down the stairs, through the entrance hall, down the back hall, and round the corner to the upper kitchen and an open door Peebs hadn't seen before. It was the distillery cupboard. Various vats of things in the process of being pickled, bottled, fermented or preserved were kept in this little cupboard, everything from onions and pickles to cleaning solutions and boot polish. Mr Franklin raised his hand in an in-you-go fashion, and Peebs reluctantly complied. It was only when the door closed behind him, and the lock clicked into place, that Peebs noticed the distillery had no window, and that it was suddenly very dark.

"Ah," he said to no one in particular. Clearly, achieving his aims in this house was going to be more difficult than he had imagined.

Peebs being now conveniently locked in the distillery cupboard, the girls were ready for Miss Verdigris's arrival. Anna brought tea to the downstairs parlour, which rarely saw any use these days, with the baroness in the country.

And by three o'clock, the three girls sat in the tall

white parlour—with its long curtains of crimson velvet, thick gold frames bearing small, dark paintings of presumably dead people, and very little clutter—taking stock of one another.

Mary thought Rebecca Verdigris was very well turned out. She was poised, and her hair was set in careful curls, and her dress was both fashionable and tasteful, and her manners were ladylike.

Ada looked at her as if she were some undiscovered species of sea creature mysteriously washed ashore.

"I don't mean to sound anxious," said Rebecca to the girls, "but when do I get to meet the Wollstonecraft detectives? This is a matter of some urgency."

"Oh," said Ada. "That's us."

"Us?" asked Rebecca politely.

"Wollstonecraft. Us. Me and Mary."

"Miss Verdigris," offered Mary, concerned at the return of Ada's choppy sentences. "I realize this is unusual—"

"Please do forgive me for interrupting, but are you quite certain that the two of you in this room are in fact the Wollstonecraft detectives?"

"Yes, entirely certain," reassured Mary.

"And," continued Rebecca, "you'll hopefully not

consider me rude for enquiring whether either of you has ever done this sort of thing before?"

"Well," answered Mary slowly, "not in so many . . ."

"Not really," said Ada curtly. "But I'm terribly clever."

"I see," said Rebecca, who began to cry. Mary fetched her a handkerchief.

"No, honestly," stated Ada. "I'm terribly clever. Everybody says so. What are you doing?"

"I'm crying," said Rebecca, through tears.

"Why? Didn't you hear the part about me being clever?"

"What Lady Ada is saying," explained Mary, "is that we're certain we can solve whatever problem faces you and put your worries to rest." Mary paused for breath to offer Rebecca a moment to collect herself. "Perhaps you can begin at the beginning."

"This concerns the events of Saturday evening," began Rebecca.

"Your coming-out party," said Ada.

"My party, yes," said Rebecca. "How did you know?"

"It was in the newspaper," said Ada. "And someone has stolen your acorn."

"How could you possibly know that?" asked Rebecca.

"It was in the newspaper. It said you were to be

presented with the Acorn of Ankara on your birth-day. And now you tell us a precious object has been stolen—it could not have been clearer."

Mary and Rebecca both blinked at Ada, a bit stunned. Mary recovered first. "Rebecca, please tell us about that night, won't you?"

"Yes. Right. My late uncle left me a necklace in his will, to be given to me upon my sixteenth birthday. He was an adventurer before he met his fate, and he acquired a pendant in the form of an acorn, which was his gift to me."

"And someone stole it," said Ada.

"Indeed, as I have said. That very night. It was in our family safe, had been for years, awaiting my coming-out. And that evening the acorn was placed around my neck by my fiancé, Mr Datchery—"

"You are to be married?" interrupted Mary.

"Yes, that's what 'fiancé' means."

"At sixteen?"

"That would be how old I am, yes," explained Rebecca, more calmly than she felt.

Mary supposed, being fourteen, that her own coming-out would be less than two years away, at which point she would be introduced to society and expected to entertain offers of marriage. At once, all concern for the case at hand was replaced with a feeling of dread.

"Please continue," said Ada.

"At the end of the soirée, which means 'party'—"

"I know what it means," groaned Ada.

"Very well. At the end of the soirée, I put it on my dressing table, in my bedroom. By morning, it had disappeared."

"Stolen," said Ada.

"That's correct."

"Hmm." Ada pondered only for a moment before declaring, "Your maid took it."

"Well, yes, that's what she says," said Rebecca, nodding.

"I'm sorry?" questioned a suddenly baffled Mary. "Who says?"

"Yes. My maid, Rosie Sparrow. She says she took the acorn, but I simply don't believe her."

"Did she give it back?" asked Mary.

"No, that's just it," explained Rebecca. "She confessed to stealing it, but insists that she does not know where it is, and that she cannot return it. But she confessed quite readily."

"So she must still have it," said Ada.

"No, she does not. And I don't believe she ever did."

"Why would she lie?" asked Ada, mostly to herself. "Criminals usually lie to get out of trouble, not into it."

"Rosie is no criminal, I'm sure of it. I have no explanation for her false confession, just as I have no idea as to the whereabouts of the acorn."

"Where," asked Mary, "is Rosie now?"

"In Newgate Prison! She turned herself in to the constabulary, confessed to the crime, and they've locked her up before her trial. But the constables searched her person and her room, and the rest of our house, and found nothing."

"If she's a clever criminal, they wouldn't have found anything," mumbled Ada.

"If she were a clever criminal, she wouldn't have confessed," said Mary.

"Point," agreed Ada.

"Rosie is no criminal, clever or otherwise. I keep telling you—"

"It should be fairly simple, really," interrupted Ada. "It wasn't an elephant, was it?"

"I beg your pardon?" replied Rebecca, still upset and unable to make head or tail of Ada generally.

"Acorn. Stolen, as you said. Not by an elephant, I'm assuming," continued Ada.

"No," Rebecca agreed. "Not an elephant."

"Well, then. See? Now we're getting somewhere. So a person, then?"

"Well, yes, surely."

"But not the maid."

"Rosie. Yes, not her."

"Someone in London?" asked Ada.

"Again, yes, but—"

"Ah. You see? With each answer, we come closer to a solution. That is precisely how it is to be done. There's a method to this sort of thing. We proceed with the method and arrive at the conclusion. It's all in the plan."

Rebecca looked at Mary, not sure what to make of Ada's speech, and composed herself.

Mary interjected, "What did the constabulary say?"

"They say they've caught the criminal—"

"Apprehended, they call it," added Ada.

"Apprehended the criminal and obtained a confession. They say Rosie must have sold the acorn or hidden it for later. But they're wrong. I just know it." Rebecca began a new round of tears.

"All right," said Ada. "Let us assume Rosie is no criminal. That means there's another criminal who is not Rosie and is not in prison."

"Yes," agreed Mary. "Let's assume that."

"So," continued Ada, "all that's left is to find the real criminal, find out why Rosie lied about being that criminal, find the acorn, and . . . um . . ."

"And get Rosie out of prison!" cried Rebecca.

"Yes, well, I knew there was another thing. I have to meet all the variables."

"Variables?" Rebecca asked.

"In the equation," Ada replied.

"She means," explained Mary, "the people. In the house. Who else was in the house that night? Who else might have taken the necklace?"

"Oh. Well, usually there's just my mother and me, but my late uncle's friend Mr Abernathy and, of course, Mr Datchery were staying with us that night. They've both remained, as I've been so upset about the theft . . ."

"What about your other servants?" asked Mary. "Besides Rosie?"

"I just can't believe *anyone* in the house was involved! And the constabulary cleared the other servants after they searched and the necklace couldn't be found . . ."

"Well, one of them took it," Ada said bluntly.

"We really should meet everyone involved," Mary added to soften the blow.

"But how shall I explain why two strange girls are asking people in my house about the crime?" asked Rebecca.

It was a good question. Mary was suddenly reminded that they were meant to be a *secret* constabulary. Perhaps they should—

"We're doing it for a school project," said Ada.

"Do you even go to school?" asked Rebecca.

"No. We don't have projects either."

Mary looked at Ada, who seemed perfectly matter-of-fact about the whole thing, and at Rebecca, who obviously did not. Somehow, a path ahead must be cleared from Rebecca's distress to Ada's certainty. What was an exercise to Ada and an adventure to Mary was a heartbreak for Rebecca. It was the time of saying *Are we absolutely sure about this?* but it was also, and more so, the time of thinking it very loudly and not saying it.

"I don't think grown-ups ask a lot of questions when you give them simple answers," Mary offered instead, which seemed to do the trick.

"Very well, then," said Rebecca, drying her tears. "We'd best be off."

VERDIGRIS MANOR

11

The words "long" and "dark", said over and over, would give a pretty good description of the Verdigris dining room. At one end of the long, dark table, and beneath a long, dark painting of a man with a long, dark expression, sat a number of actual nonpainting people with matching long, dark expressions.

"It is unfortunate, but the criminal has been apprehended," said Lady Verdigris sternly. Lady Verdigris was Rebecca's mother, dressed all in black with buttons up to her chin, and Mary could not imagine her saying or doing anything in a way that could not be described as "sternly".

"Mama, no!" insisted Rebecca. "I've known Rosie since we were girls. She's no criminal!"

Behind Rebecca stood a handsome young man in a lavender frock coat. He said nothing, but placed his hands reassuringly on Rebecca's shoulders, and so Mary assumed this must be Mr Datchery, Rebecca's fiancé. Lady Verdigris gave the young man a stern look, and he took his hands away and put them behind his back.

Standing behind the stern Lady Verdigris was an oddly shaped man, thin but with a round belly (which made him look somehow thin and fat at the same time) and a sort of pear-shaped head with a long, narrow nose.

The oddly shaped man had introduced himself as a Mr Abernathy, a wealthy friend of the family.

"I'm a wealthy friend of the family," he had said. "Very rich. Friendly."

Mary found it particularly rude of him to mention that he was rich, as in her experience the people with the most money never seemed to bring it up at all.

Mary watched Ada watch the four people at the

end of the table: the stern Lady Verdigris, the upset Rebecca, the oddly shaped Abernathy, and the comforting young man. The variables.

"And who is he?" asked Ada, forgetting they had been introduced. It was the first time she had spoken in the Verdigris house. Ada had seemed overwhelmed by the outing, by being outside in general, and had clutched Mary's hand tightly when they left the carriage and entered the house.

"I am Beau Datchery, Lady Ada. Miss Verdigris's fiancé. We were introduced not moments ago."

"Did you take it?"

"I'm sorry? Did I take what?" said Beau, confused.

"The acorn. Pendant. Thingy," said Ada.

"And you say this is for a school project?" questioned Lady Verdigris. Ada ignored her and continued to question Beau.

"Well, certainly Rebecca didn't take it, because she already had it in her possession. Lady Verdigris didn't take it, because she had it before, in the safe, waiting to give it to Rebecca. Mr Angrybunny—"

"Abernathy," said Mr Abernathy.

"Him. You. You didn't take it because you don't need it, because you're rich. You said so. Twice.

And Rosie didn't take it, or at least Rebecca says so. And all your other servants have been cleared by the constables?"

"Of course!" Lady Verdigris huffed.

"So that leaves the fiancé." Ada turned to Beau. "I'm afraid you're the only one left. Therefore, you took it. And not an elephant." She nodded smugly to Rebecca.

Beau was quite surprised by this and didn't seem to know what to say. So he said "Um" instead.

"Lady Ada," said Rebecca reassuringly. "Beau did not need to take the acorn. If he desired it, I simply would have given it to him. And when we are married, anything that belongs to me will belong to him."

"Will it?" asked Ada.

"Yes, it shall."

"Well, that doesn't make any sense to me," said Ada.

"Nevertheless," added Lady Verdigris, which annoyed Ada greatly. "While I'm sure this is very educational"—she stressed the word—"the matter is dealt with. The maid has confessed. The pendant is unrecoverable."

"Might I ask if there's a drawing or something?"

asked Mary. "So we know what it looks like? For our, er, school project."

"There's an entire book on it," stated Lady Verdigris. "Geoffrey, do you have Colonel Havisham's book?"

Geoffrey was apparently Mr Abernathy's first name, and he did have Colonel Havisham's book. He handed a small green clothbound volume to Mary, somewhat reluctantly. She thanked him, and when Ada reached for it out of habit, Mary had to give Ada a "not now" look—twice, as Ada missed it the first time—and then she finally relented, handing it over for Ada's examination.

The book was travel-worn and tatty, with the image of a gold acorn embossed on the cover. Beneath the acorn, in a ribbon, it read *De parvis grandis acervus erit,* which Ada knew was Latin, although she didn't know what it meant. She noted that the book smelled very faintly of fish.

"This was written by my good friend Colonel Havisham, now deceased," explained Abernathy. "It tells of his adventures in Turkey, where he acquired the jewel."

"Do you mind if we borrow this?" asked Mary.

"Of course you may," said Rebecca. "Anything to help. Your, er, school project." The expression on Rebecca's face was at once hopeful and sad.

Mary made her thanks and polite excuses, and the Wollstonecraft girls followed the Verdigrises' butler (who was both short and talkative) to the front door.

As they approached the waiting carriage, Ada seemed to forget her anxiety, her mind busy with the details of the case. "Excellent. Now there are only two things left to do," she said with confidence.

Mary was momentarily distracted by the sight of three unusual men standing across the street. Men wearing odd, flat-topped caps of red felt, like upturned flowerpots. Men who seemed to be staring directly at her. She found the feeling quite unnerving.

"Two?" asked Mary, her attention returning to Ada.

"One, read this book," said Ada, holding it up in one gloved hand. "And two, go to prison."

As Mary climbed into the black carriage, half

expecting to see a boy pretending not to be there, her heart began to flutter at the thought of danger and adventure. Prison? Ada couldn't be serious. But, of course, Ada was as serious as Mr Abernathy was oddly shaped, and as serious as Lady Verdigris was stern. They would have to interview Rosie and ask why she confessed to something Rebecca was sure she didn't do. And that meant getting into prison. Somehow.

"Hello?" said Peebs, still locked in the distillery cupboard back at the Marylebone house. "I have to go to the bathroom."

OMNIBUS

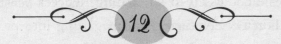

12

Ada was stepping from the carriage into the cobbled road across from the Byron house when without warning the horse reared, and the carriage lurched, and Ada, who still had one foot aboard, pitched forward. Mary's hand shot out and caught her, pulling her back inside just as a team of three horses abreast bolted past them, hauling the longest carriage the girls had ever seen. They had never imagined anything quite so large moving quite so fast. Had Mary not caught Ada, if she had fallen, she would surely have been killed.

The girls caught their breath and waited until the enormous contraption was well past them before stepping together into the road.

"Good heavens! What on earth was that?" asked Mary of the coachman.

"That'd be the omnibus, miss," he told her. "Three horses, and twenty-seven aboard. Biggest beast the streets of London have ever seen."

"Lady Ada could have been killed," Mary stated plainly.

"The bus don't seem to care, do it?" the coachman replied. Realizing this sounded harsh, he added, "I'm sorry, miss. I do hope she's all right. That thing is a monster, and shouldn't be allowed on the streets. Gives ol' Charlie here an awful fright each time." Mary guessed ol' Charlie was the carriage horse, and she suddenly felt quite sorry for him. She smiled and gave them both—coachman and Charlie—a little curtsy, then took Ada's hand firmly as they crossed the street to the house.

Greatly unsettled by her brush with death, Ada climbed automatically up the stairs to her balloon while Mary headed to the drawing room to make notes from their interview with the Verdigris family.

Passing the library, she noticed a recently released Peebs hurriedly replacing a small blue book on a shelf.

"Ah," he said, nervous about something. "Miss Godwin. You're back."

"Yes, thank you," said Mary, not sure what she was thanking him for.

"I'll just, um, yes. Books. Many, many books."

"This is the library," said Mary calmly.

"Yes. Just, you know, browsing. No particular book. Just books in general."

"I often enjoy browsing books. In general."

"Yes, well, that's quite enough browsing for me now. If you'll excuse me," he said, hurrying past her.

Mary had a sneaking suspicion creeping deliciously up her spine and into her head. This particular sneaking suspicion had to do with a small blue book, and Peebs's talking about books in general so as to distract her from that specific small blue book in particular. She decided to investigate.

There were several blue books on the shelf that Peebs had just been browsing, but only one was exactly the right amount of small and exactly the right shade of blue. She was tall for her age, and only had to tiptoe a little bit to reach it.

93

The book was oddly familiar, and it only took a heartbeat to realize that she had an identical copy in her own family library at home. The book was a collection of stories for children called *Original Stories from Real Life; with Conversations, Calculated to Regulate the Affections, and Form the Mind to Truth and Goodness*, by Mary Wollstonecraft. Her mother. She actually had two copies at home—a rather plain one, which had her mother's scribbles in the margins, and this one, with illustrations by a Mr William Blake. Unscribbled.

A certain chill of excitement took Mary as she opened the book to read the inscription:

> *To my dear friend George (Albé)*
> *on the birth of his daughter Allegra 1817*
> *"Hail to thee, blithe sprit!"*
> *Yours as ever, PBS (Shiloh)*

Mary covered her mouth as though she meant to scream but must not. "George" had to be Ada's father, Lord Byron, and "PBS", of course, was Peebs. Mary didn't know about an Allegra—Ada had never mentioned a sister—but based on the year, Ada would

94

have been (some quick maths) two when this inscription was written.

But there was the secret. That was why Peebs had been trying to be clandestine in the library.

Mother won't talk about him. She won't let his books in the house. His friends used to come to visit, but she shooed them away, said Ada in Mary's memory.

Peebs had been a friend of Ada's father's, and Ada's father's friends were forbidden in the Byron house. The Baroness Wentworth, as Ada had explained, had gone to great lengths to keep her husband's former associates from having anything to do with the family, especially with Ada herself.

Peebs was a spy.

This idea both delighted and horrified Mary. How exciting! How dangerous! Should she confront Peebs on the matter? Would the secret revealed mean that Peebs would no longer be a tutor in the house? If Peebs were no longer a tutor, would Mary be sent off to school? Could Mary and Ada still be friends? What of the Wollstonecraft Detective Agency? What was meant by "Albé" and "Shiloh"? Did Ada really have a secret sister?

So many questions. Mary counted seven off the

top of her head, and so many questions made her want to sit down until she realized she had already sat down on the floor without bothering to notice.

It was a good floor, with broad wooden boards and an ornate rug atop, and Mary was grateful for it. The floor sat there holding up the entire library, as well as Mary herself, and it didn't ask any questions.

Mary stared resolutely at the cover of the book. What would her mother tell her to do, if she were there? The right thing. Of course, the right thing. But what was it?

After a good sit, Mary understood that the right thing was to tell Ada what she knew—but after she had given Peebs a chance to explain. Perhaps Ada wouldn't mind that Peebs had somehow smuggled himself into the Byron house, like a stowaway, under false pretences, like a spy. Whether Ada minded or not was Ada's decision, and not Mary's, and Mary sighed at the truth of that. Even if it meant the end of her tutoring, and the end of the friendship, and no end to the mystery of the missing Verdigris acorn, she could not keep the truth from her friend.

As she stood upon the firm and trustworthy floor,

she set out to confront Peebs with her discovery so that they could share the truth with Ada together.

But then the great knocker on the front door sounded and the clock in the hall chimed, which meant that a carriage had arrived to take Mary home to Somers Town.

The truth would have to wait until morning.

RIBBON
AND NEWDOG

13

Mary scarcely said a word to Charles the next morning, which was just as well, as he continued to pretend he wasn't there. He'd made no enquiry as to the Wollstonecraft Detective Agency, despite being the one who actually placed the advertisement in the newspaper and delivered all the missives. She couldn't tell if he was uninterested or just really good at being clandestine.

She felt that there was a balloon in her chest, squished somewhere between her breastbone and her heart, that grew ever so slightly larger with each passing moment.

Peebs is a spy, it whispered until Mary found it hard to breathe.

When the carriage arrived at the Marylebone house, Mary opened the door slowly, checked for the galloping threat of the omnibus, and bade Charles a good morning, expecting no reply. The door was suddenly yanked open by Ada, in a cape and bonnet, who climbed in as though she were expected. Mary could see Mr Franklin on the doorstep, seeing Ada safely away.

"Who is he?" asked Ada, pointedly staring at Charles.

"Please don't speak to me. I'm not supposed to be here, so I'm pretending I'm not," said Charles from behind his book.

Ada nodded.

"So that's you, then," she said, and began pretending that Charles wasn't there. It astonished Mary how easily Ada accepted things once she was given what she considered to be a reasonable explanation.

"What do we know," stated Ada in her not-a-question-but-really-a-question voice.

We know Peebs is a spy, whispered the squishy balloon in Mary's chest, and Mary wanted to let it out. But she knew that the right thing to do, the only right thing, was to give Peebs the chance to explain himself first.

"What do we know about what?" asked Mary, pretending not to understand.

"The case. Rebecca. Honestly, Mary, do try."

"Well," said Mary, trying to wrap her head around things, "Rebecca Verdigris is sixteen and engaged to a Mr Beau Datchery, and she inherited a pendant from her uncle, Colonel Something."

"Havisham," said Ada.

"Tell me, how is it that you recall the name of a dead relative in a case we found out about yesterday, yet you cannot remember the name of a maid who's been living in your house for years?"

"He wrote a book," said Ada. "It smells like fish. Go on."

"Um, all right. There's Lady Verdigris . . ."

"Go back. How do we know Rebecca didn't take the acorn?"

"Because she already owned it."

"Precisely. Go on."

"Right. There's Lady Verdigris, Rebecca's mother. She's a bit of a cold fish, if you ask me."

"I didn't see anything wrong with her," said Ada.

"I didn't say there was something wrong with her. She was just a bit . . ."

"What?"

"Stern," said Mary.

"And we know Lady Verdigris didn't take it because . . ." continued Ada.

"Is that a question?" asked Mary.

"Yes."

"You know, it's rather difficult to tell sometimes."

"Mmm" was all that Ada had to contribute.

"Fine," Mary carried on. "We know Lady Verdigris did not steal the acorn because it was in her possession all this time. She had it. And she gave it to Rebecca. If she wanted it that badly, she could have kept it for herself and not even bothered to tell Rebecca about it."

"Very good," said Ada. "And Mr Allthemoney."

"Abernathy."

"Him."

"Well, you said he didn't take it, because he was rich. He kept saying so, which was rather odd," added Mary.

"Was it?"

"Well, you know more rich people than I do. But I don't think they mention how rich they are all the time."

"Do I?" asked Ada.

"Do I what?" said Mary, meaning to say "you" instead.

"Do I know more rich people than you?"

"You're *gentry*, Ada. *Lady* Ada. That usually means rich, and knowing rich people."

"What are you?"

"Whatever do you mean?" asked Mary, surprised.

"If I'm gentry, and you're not, what are you?"

"I'm just a girl, silly."

After a brief silence, Ada returned to the case. "The fiancé."

"Well, we don't know much about Mr Datchery, except that Rebecca is clearly in love with him," stated Mary.

"She is?"

"She is. I could tell."

"How?"

"I just . . . could tell. There are some things you just know, and this is one of them."

Ada sat again in silence for a moment. "Did her eyes get bigger?"

"Whose?"

"Rebecca's."

"I didn't notice."

"I'll look, next time."

Mary wondered about this. "What would that mean, if her eyes got bigger?"

"I'm working on a theory," said Ada. "How do we know he didn't take it?"

"Well, Rebecca said that after they were married, Beau would own it anyway."

"That seems odd."

"That's marriage, Ada."

"Well, I'm filing it under 'odd' anyway. Havisham," said Ada, like a funny sneeze.

"Bless you."

"No. Havisham. What do we know?"

"He was Rebecca's uncle, he's dead, he left her the acorn in his will as a birthday present. That's all I know."

Ada began to wander the hallways of her brain: "Oliver Hypotenuse Havisham, Colonel. Officer and adventurer. There's a plate, copper thingy, a picture of him, holding the necklace." There was a sailor in the background of the picture—oddly shaped enough to be Havisham's wealthy friend, she thought, but he reminded her too of someone she couldn't place.

Ada continued. "He spent most of his career in Turkey, where he acquired the Acorn of Ankara, a Turkish 'national treasure' said to have the property of mesmerism. That was in the book."

"How does one 'acquire' a national treasure of somewhere else?"

"I think it means he just took it away with him."

"That's hardly polite. He seems rather a scoundrel, gentleman or no. What's mesmerism?" asked Mary.

"I have absolutely no idea. The word isn't in the dictionary."

"There are words that aren't in the dictionary?"

"Yes, they're still working on it. When I find a word that isn't in there, I find out what it means and send it to them."

"To whom?" asked Mary, baffled.

"To the dictionary."

"You could ask—" Mary started. *The spy,* she thought. "Peebs," she finished, after a moment.

"Mmm," said Ada again. "Possibly. We also know

that Havisham was the brother of Lady Verdigris and a friend of Mr Abudabbi."

"Abernathy."

"Him."

At this, the carriage stopped. Mary hadn't asked where they were, or where they were going.

"Pardon me. Boot-polish factory," said Charles, closing his book. "I glue the labels on." He pulled a cap out of his pocket and put it on, tipped the brim, and opened the door to one of the many less pleasant parts of London.

Ada didn't bother to say goodbye, seeing as he wasn't actually even there in the first place, officially speaking.

"Where are we going?" asked Mary.

"There's one person in the case we have yet to meet. Except for Havisham, but he's dead, so that's difficult. We're here for the maid."

Mary had had a sneaking suspicion, of course, but she didn't like this one as much.

"So we really are going to prison," she said.

"That's where the not-clever criminals are," said Ada, nodding. "We can't use our real names, as we are secret detectives. We'll have to be clandestine."

"Yes! Though I suppose it would have been better had we used clandestine names at Verdigris Manor . . ."

"Mmm," Ada acknowledged.

"Well, whatever shall we—"

"I," said Ada, "shall be Miss Ribbon, and you can be Miss Newdog."

"Newdog?"

"It's sort of an anagram."

"What's an anagram?" asked Mary.

"A letter scramble. Your last name is Godwin, and that's Niwdog backwards, so it's close enough to Newdog. You can remember it that way."

"And Miss Ribbon?"

"Well, Byron backwards is Noryb, and that's silly, and Ribbon is easier to remember."

"It would," agreed Mary, "be less clandestine if we were unable to remember our own names."

Mary found the idea of having a clandestine name exciting, although secretly she wished for one more glamorous than Newdog.

And then they were there, at the front of the worst place in the world.

NEWGATE

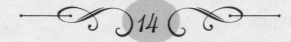

14

Its rough, heavy walls and low, massive doors looked like they were designed for letting people in and then never letting them out again. Newgate Prison.

A guard box, painted a gleaming black, was posted outside the terrifying entrance. In the box stood a man in a blue cape, who Mary assumed must have been tired, as there was no stool inside for him to sit down on. There was a fire grate propped on three legs, with a small, greasy fire within, but it seemed just ever so slightly too far from the guard box to offer any comfort.

The girls left the carriage; Ada paid the coachman extra to wait for them, however long it took, and they approached the guard box.

Ada stopped in the middle of the road, between coach and black shelter.

"I've just remembered something important," she said.

"What's that?" Mary asked.

"I don't like this."

"I'm sorry? You don't like what, Ada?"

"Outside. Being. Not in the house." Ada was frozen as if bolted to the road, her choppy manner of speech returning.

"I'm sure you'll be fine," comforted Mary.

"I won't. Can't move my feet. Can't breathe."

Mary thought for a moment, concerned. "Ada? If you couldn't breathe, you couldn't speak."

Ada seemed to relax. "That makes sense."

"You just need to keep your wits about you," clucked Mary. "Concentrate on the next step. First we must get out of the road before we're run down. And we have to get in *there* somehow. We'll need a story."

"Whatever for?"

"We can't just wander in and ask to look about. It's Newgate Prison. We don't belong in there."

"We could say we're impoverished orphans. There was a story in the newspaper about impoverished orphans that had Peebs all upset. And people who wrote to the paper after said the story was quite touching."

"Ada . . ."

"Although I'm not sure what it was touching, exactly. I mean, possibly your eyeballs. Or your thumbs. You do often use your thumbs to touch the newspaper, and then they get all smudgy from the ink."

"Ada!"

"Mmm?"

"Look at that gentleman in the guard box. The cost of your bonnet could feed his family for a fortnight. You make a very unconvincing impoverished orphan."

"Really? Well, I suppose I could get a different bonnet."

"I don't think that's going to work."

"Fine," declared Ada. "Then we'll do it my way." And she marched purposefully towards the guard box, pleased to have a problem she could solve.

"Open the door," said Ada to the guard.

"Beggin' your pardon, miss?" replied the guard.

"Open the door. Please. We'd like to go in."

"Well, that's very curious indeed, miss. Folk don't often ask to get in. It's the wanting to get out that you usually hear about."

"In which case," continued Ada, "letting us in can hardly be a problem, can it?"

"Putting it that way, miss," said the guard, "I s'pose it's all right, then." And he twisted the heavy black iron ring on the enormous door, the latches sliding back with a *ker-clunk,* like the loading of cannons.

Ada gave a little nod and marched into the darkness beyond the giant door, utterly fearless. Mary trotted along behind her in astonishment, nearly tripping herself as she gave a running curtsy to the guard.

"That was really terribly clever," said Mary. "How do you plan to get out again?"

"I can hardly be expected to think of everything," replied Ada.

And the door swung shut behind them, with the cannon *ker-clunk* letting them know they were locked in.

Mary saw a dim corridor before them. At the end

of the corridor, the hallway split in two directions. There were no signs and no prison guards they could ask for directions.

"How are we to find Rosie in here?"

Ada pointed to the right. "This way."

"How do you know?" asked Mary.

"I don't. I'm just guessing. But if I'm wrong, the other way will still be there."

They proceeded down the right-hand corridor. The gloom was thick, almost sticky with sorrow and defeat and other unpleasantness. Mary could feel a sadness creeping into her bones. She began to make out the sounds of prisoners in their grim cells: scraping and whistling, snoring or crying. She could hear coughing and moaning and a horrid squelching sound she couldn't begin to identify. She suddenly realized she'd been walking alone for a few paces, Ada no longer beside her. She turned round.

"Ada?"

Ada was rooted to the floor of the hallway. "Really don't want to be here, I remembered."

"I don't think anybody wants to be here."

"Feet not working again."

"But they were working just fine a moment ago."

"Then I remembered. About the not wanting to be here."

Mary nodded. She had to keep Ada moving, as Mary had little desire to be here much longer herself.

"Well, to get out of here, you're going to need your feet."

"That makes sense."

"And it's not as bad as last time, when you said you couldn't breathe, but could."

"Mmm."

"So you were mistaken about your breathing then, and you might well be mistaken about your feet now. Take a step and see."

"That's a good experiment," said Ada nervously, taking a step.

"Any conclusions?" asked Mary.

"Feet work."

"Right. Well, let's use them to get us to Rosie, find out what we need, and get out of here."

Taking Ada's hand, Mary led them back the way they had come, and they tried the other hallway, hoping it might prove more promising. It was equally awful, and thick with misery. Each step seemed harder to take than the last, and again Ada stopped.

Then she shouted at the top of her lungs, *"ROSIE!!"* and the cry was an explosion, an avalanche down the chilly hall. It was met by the sound of nothing.

"I'm curious as to how that could have been expected to work," said Mary, after a bit.

Ada shrugged.

But then, in the lingering silence, they heard a very small "Yes?"

ROSIE SPARROW

15

"Rosie?" asked Mary. "Rosie Sparrow?"

The maid seemed to wake slowly, although she'd been sitting up and her eyes were wet with tears.

"Yes?" she said quietly.

"Rosie, we're . . . um, Misses . . ."

"Ribbon and Newdog," said Ada.

"We're friends of Miss Rebecca's," Mary continued. "She has asked us to find out why you confessed to a crime you did not commit."

"Miss Rebecca asked you . . . ?" murmured Rosie, as though from a distance.

"She knows in her heart you are innocent," Mary persevered. "Tell me, did you take the acorn?"

"The acorn," repeated the imprisoned maid.

"The pendant. Her birthday gift. Did you take it?"

"I said I did," replied Rosie.

"We know that already," huffed Ada.

Mary shot her a look, but Ada missed it. "Yes, Rosie, we are aware of what you *said* you did. But I must beg of you to trust us. Miss Rebecca wants you to trust us. We know you didn't *actually do* it, did you?"

"No," said Rosie quietly.

"There. And I believe you. Now, whyever would you confess to taking the acorn when you did not?"

Rosie looked like she was about to return to the tears she had been crying before the girls arrived.

"It would break my Rebecca's heart for her to know the truth," she blurted suddenly.

"But, Rosie," assured Mary. "It is breaking her heart to know that you are here, in prison, when you've done nothing wrong."

"She *has* done something wrong," said Ada. "She lied to the constabulary, lied to her friend and her employer, and kept the real criminal out of the newspaper. Prison."

"Ada!"

"Ribbon!" corrected Ada.

"That's a terrible thing to say," rebuked Mary.

"It's not a good thing to do either," said Ada angrily. "It doesn't make any sense."

"Are you suggesting," said Mary to Rosie, "that if Rebecca found out who really took the acorn, it would be worse for her than it is knowing that you're here in this awful place?"

Rosie fought the urge to cry, and nodded.

"So all of this is to save Rebecca's feelings?"

Rosie sniffed, and nodded again.

"Beau," said Mary quietly.

"Told you," added Ada.

"What? How do you—? Please, you mustn't tell Miss Rebecca," begged Rosie. "She loves him so, and it would break her heart if she knew Mr Datchery was the thief."

"But I don't understand," said Mary. "As her friend, wouldn't you want to stop her from marrying a bad man?"

117

"That's just it," replied Rosie. "He is not a bad man. He's a very good man. I don't know what could've possibly possessed him to steal the pendant, but I saw him do it. While everyone was downstairs, I saw him coming out of Rebecca's room. I gasped, I was that shocked, but he never noticed. He had the necklace in his hand—he just carried it down the hallway, staring at it the whole time like it was something from his dreams. Then next morning when Rebecca discovered it was missing, I told her I had stolen it. She'd be crushed to find he took it. And there'd be such a scandal. And think of Mr Datchery's reputation."

"If he stole it, he's a criminal, and *he* should be in here and not you," said Ada. Somehow, the iron bars reminded her of the lines between the narrow columns in the newspaper, and the grey stone reminded her of the pages themselves. Grim, but tidy.

"It would break Miss Rebecca's heart if the man she loved were here."

"It's breaking her heart that *you* are here," countered Mary. "Rosie, what if we can find a way to solve this riddle? There must be some explanation, and if we can find it, then we can restore the acorn, present the explanation, and get you out of this dreadful place."

For the first time, Rosie smiled. She nodded and wiped a tear. "I dared not hope that such a thing were possible."

"Well, I'm certain it is possible. Ada, I mean, Miss Ribbon here, is extremely clever, and I've no doubt she will get to the bottom of this."

"Thank you," said Rosie. "Thank you ever so . . ."

Mary squeezed Rosie's hands through the bars.

Memory served as their guide out of the dungeon, back towards the dim cavern behind the stout front doors. Mary gave the oak a sharp, desperate knock, which reverberated through the shadows of the prison.

The door opened a crack, and welcome daylight rushed into the hall.

"Can I help you?" asked the man from the guard box.

"It's us. We came in, and we'd like to come out again," said Ada.

"Well, I can't just go letting people out of prison, can I?"

"And whyever not?"

"Lose me job, I would. What kind of a prison guard would I be if I let people out all willy-nilly?"

"Not a very good one, I imagine," admitted Mary. "But we're . . ."

"Yes?"

"Impoverished orphans," said Mary with some desperation.

"You don't look it," said the guard.

"Thank you. Now please let us out."

"No, sorry. You need a letter of release from the magistrate before I can let you out. And I don't see too many o' them, at that—you've got to be Lord or Lady Such-and-Such to even ask for one. That's how it works."

"But you just let us in."

"In is one thing. Out needs paperwork."

Ada concentrated, remembering bits from her newspaper reading. "And do you have a warrant?" she asked.

"Begging your pardon, miss?"

"A warrant. For our arrest. I've read all about them, and we can't be here without a warrant. Have you got one?"

"But I don't know who you are, so how can I know if there's a warrant for you?"

"Well, there's no sense in asking us," said Ada. "If

we were criminals, we'd simply lie about our names so that the warrants wouldn't match and you'd have to let us out."

"Interesting point, miss. In that case, I'll have to keep you in."

Mary was starting to panic at the thought of remaining on the wrong side of this heavy and forbidding door. "Impoverished orphans!" she repeated.

"The fact remains," stated Ada calmly, "that you have no warrant for our arrest, and as you have us imprisoned here, I am afraid we will have to call the constabulary."

"But I *am* the constabulary, miss."

"Very well. Then I shall ask you to consider yourself under arrest and place yourself in prison."

The guard was quite surprised and quite confused. "Under arrest? Myself? What for?"

"Kidnapping, clearly," said Ada. "Here you are, keeping two impoverished orphans locked up, without so much as a warrant. That's a crime, and you're a constable. You're supposed to arrest criminals, so you'd best get to it."

"Steady on," said the poor guard. "That doesn't seem quite—"

"You're IMPOSSIBLE!" shouted Ada, getting truly angry. "There's a KIDNAPPING going on and you're just STANDING there! Aren't you going to stop it? You're supposed to be a constable!"

"I—I don't quite know how, exactly," stammered the man.

Ada rolled her eyes and stamped her foot, and she was very, very good at it. "You let us go, is how, exactly," she said curtly.

"Ah, yes, well, that does seem to make sense," admitted the guard, grateful for a way out of this hopelessly confusing situation.

Ada glared at the man, and then at his hand on the door ring, and back at him, her eyes flashing menace. With an "Erm," he opened the door wider, allowing the young detectives to escape the prison and inhale deeply the air of the wonderful, filthy, soggy London street.

Outside was most definitely, perfectly better than inside.

THE
FISHMONGER

16

Across the road, the waiting coach seemed a refuge. Mary resisted the urge to run for it.

She walked sedately, holding Ada's hand, even pausing politely to let a cluster of nuns scurry by. Then a curious shape caught her eye. In fact, it was three curious shapes, or one curious shape repeated three times. Three red fezzes, like upturned flowerpots, worn by men not looking at each other, and whistling.

"Don't look," cautioned Mary, entering the carriage.

"Don't look at what?" asked Ada.

"Three men, trying to look inconspicuous." She cast an inquisitive look at Ada and regretted it instantly.

"I *know* what 'inconspicuous' means. You see three men trying hard not to be seen. They're obviously not very good at being inconspicuous."

"I'm sorry, I forget that you know everything. Except your maid's name."

"Chuzzlewit?" offered Ada.

"Cumberland. Honestly, Ada, nobody is named Chuzzlewit."

"And mesmerism. I don't know what that is."

"Not yet." After a pause, Mary added, "I've seen them before."

"Who?"

"Whom," corrected Mary.

"Whom?"

"The three men in red fezzes, trying to be inconspicuous. They were watching us outside the Verdigris mansion."

"Did they look like criminals?" asked Ada.

"I don't think so—they were very well dressed."

Ada didn't know much about men's fashion, and left it to Mary to decide if the men in red fezzes really

were well dressed or not. Ada dared a glance out of the rear carriage window as they drove off, and indeed there they were: three finely turned-out gentlemen in red fezzes. One wore a sort of lapel pin or medal that flashed a sunburst as best as it was able in the autumn gloom. She turned back to Mary, hoping they hadn't seen her looking.

"They might be well-dressed criminals," Ada suggested.

"I'm sure that's possible. But do you think they're *our* criminals?" Mary asked.

"I doubt it. Rosie has already told us that Beau is the criminal. Besides, if the three men in red fezzes had the acorn, I can't imagine why they would be following us. They must want it and are hoping we'll find it."

"You read the book. Is it valuable?"

"The book?" asked Ada.

"No, silly, the acorn."

"Oh. I don't know. It's not a diamond or anything. It's a moonstone. Sodium potassium aluminium silicate. It is extremely ancient, from Ankara in Turkey, and aside from its powers of mesmerism—and we don't even know what that means—it's just . . ."

"Just what?"

"Pretty," decided Ada.

"Pretty! I don't think I've ever heard you call anything that," said Mary in surprise. "Anyway, Turkey sounds terribly exotic. I'd love to travel there someday."

"We should go and tell Rebecca about Beau," said Ada, changing the subject.

"Well," said Mary carefully, being reminded of Peebs the spy. "This is a delicate situation. The right thing to do would be to give Beau a chance to explain himself, and then we can present the facts to Rebecca."

"Why?"

"Because," Mary said guiltily, "sometimes you need to be careful about what you say and when you say it."

"That's silly. There are just things to know, and people should know them and that's that."

At this, the guilty, squishy balloon in Mary's chest swelled to the point where she had trouble breathing.

It was a very short carriage ride between Newgate Prison and the Marylebone house, barely two and a half miles, a fact Mary found unsettling. As large as London was, the greatest city in the world, it seemed not quite large enough, being so close to so horrible a place.

As Ada paid the coachman, Mary suddenly remembered something. Peebs. Not the terrible secret that weighed so heavily on her heart, but Peebs the tutor, who would have been expecting the girls in the drawing room over an hour ago.

"Peebs!" she cried. "However shall we explain ourselves?"

"Oh, don't worry about him," said Ada, climbing down. "I had Mr Franklin lock him in the distillery cupboard again."

"Again? What do you mean 'again'?" asked Mary, aghast.

"Like yesterday."

"Ada! You simply cannot go around locking people in distillery cupboards!"

"Fine. He can be in the pantry tomorrow. Besides, I'm sure he's out by now."

As the girls were unexpected, there was no Mr Franklin at the door to greet them, and Ada marched right in, the mud from her boots leaving marks on the gleaming white floor as she strode towards the upstairs kitchen.

Mary followed, thinking of poor Anna Cumberland, who would have to clean up Ada's mess once again, if "once again" meant "all the time without stopping ever".

Mary half expected to see Anna in the kitchen, or perhaps Mr Franklin or even the recently released Peebs, although Mary was sure she would prefer the distillery cupboard to Newgate Prison.

What she did not expect to see was Ada holding a very large and rather nasty-looking knife—the length of her arm—and pointing it at a total stranger in the kitchen.

"Who are you?" Ada demanded. "And what are you doing in my house?"

"Pardon me, miss. I'm just the new fishmonger." The man kept his back to Ada and unwrapped several fresh fish—kippers and skate and one red herring—from rolls of brown paper. There was even an eel glistening wetly on the counter. He spread his hands to show they were empty, and Ada caught a glimpse of a tattoo on his forearm. The letter *S,* and others, though she couldn't quite catch what they said.

"As you can see. Fish. Sorry if I frightened you. I'll be on my way, beggin' your leave." And without

turning, he left his parcels on the kitchen counter and practically fled out of the back door.

"What's a fishmonger?" asked Ada, without moving or lowering her lethal-looking knife.

"Someone who mongs fish," answered Mary, though she knew at once that wasn't right. "Sells. Delivers. Delivers fish to kitchens."

"He left his knife here."

"Is that his knife?" asked Mary, looking at the one in Ada's hand.

"No, there, by the paper."

Sure enough, beside the floppy, dead and moist eel on the counter was a long, skinny knife with a curving blade. It had a little hole at the end of the handle, and a short loop of leather was run through it.

"He must have been in quite a hurry," said Ada. "You'd think he'd need that."

"He probably thought you were going to chop his head off with that thing," said Mary.

"No, he turned round as soon as he saw me, before I picked up my knife. This knife."

"Can you please put it down? You're making me terribly nervous."

Ada put down the long butcher's knife. "There was

something familiar about him." She walked towards the fishmonger's knife and gave it a sniff.

"Well, if he's your fishmonger, perhaps you've seen him before."

"I don't think that's it. He said he was the *new* fishmonger. Smells fishy."

"I can hardly follow you, Ada. What smells fishy?"

"All of it, especially this knife."

"Well, of course it does. It's a fish knife. From a fishmonger. If it smelled like cheese, it would be unusual."

"No," said Ada. "It's this particular fishy smell that smells fishy. I recognize it, but can't remember from where."

Mary hadn't thought of it before, but while she was certain that there were many different kinds of fish, they all simply smelled fishy to her. But she had to admit that Ada's sense of smell was as sharp as the fishmonger's knife, which she held up under her nose like a curving steel moustache.

THE
TIMES

17

Thwap. Charles closed the heavy leather book with decision, but not without disappointment. The word "mesmerism" had not been in the dictionary, just as Ada had said. Mary was sure, but Charles thought there was no harm in checking.

The two stood beside a long, wood-panelled counter in the grey-walled basement beneath *The Times* office. Light came in from a series of horizontal windows set high on the wall near the ceiling, like glass envelopes onto the grey street. Tall wooden bookshelves stood in ranks that seemed to go on and on for ever below the

London streets, each square shelf stacked with ageing grey newspapers, folded like blankets. Mary found the sight a little sad, as though each newspaper, one kept for each day going back over forty years, were a book that would never again be read. She imagined they must be lonely.

Mary had left the Marylebone house the previous afternoon with an assignment. As Ada had been overwhelmed by the outing to the prison and the curious encounter with the fishmonger, after which the *entire house* seemed to smell fishy, Mary alone would do what research she could regarding the mysterious word "mesmerism". Ada would invent some excuse to Peebs for Mary's lateness.

Mary had also left with her secret still ballooning in her chest. Peebs had apparently decamped in a bit of a huff after Mr Franklin released him from his second imprisonment in the distillery cupboard, so Mary hadn't been able to talk to him about his being a spy.

Her search for the word "mesmerism" was also a puzzle.

The Times was an obvious choice, as the newspaper was in the business of knowing things, and knowing words in particular, but they were hardly going to allow a girl in by herself. Without an escort, Mary quickly realized, it would be impossible. She had entered the morning's coach desperately hoping that Charles would be officially-not-there but actually-there, as usual. And he was.

"Charles?"

"Mmm?" he replied, nose in a book as always.

"You know what you said earlier, about a damsel in distress?"

"Mmm?" he repeated.

Mary wasn't sure what to make of that, so she pressed on. "Well, I'm not certain, but I think perhaps I may be one."

He put down his book immediately.

She continued. "There is something I must do, but I cannot think of a way to do it without your help."

"No," said Charles. "Not a damsel in distress *technically*." He savoured the word. "But a friend in need, as before. What am I doing?"

Relieved, Mary clarified. "*We*. What we are doing. Together. Hunting for a word, the meaning of a word, that Miss . . . Ribbon says is not in the dictionary."

Charles shrugged. "Dr Johnson's dictionary is

quite old," he said. "Perhaps we're hunting for a new word?"

"You have it exactly!" exclaimed Mary. "I knew you'd understand. Ada suggested we go to *The Times* and look there."

"A capital plan, miss. But they won't let you in alone."

"Because I'm a girl."

"Yes."

"You know, that's not entirely fair."

"No," Charles acknowledged.

"Which is why I was hoping you would escort me. But," Mary rushed to say, "I don't need you just because you're a boy."

"No?"

"No. I need you because you know *The Times,* and you love books, which means you know words." Mary paused. "And I need you because you're my friend."

"That settles it, then," said Charles. "*The Times* it is."

The two rode all the way to Charles's boot-polish factory, where Mary waited in the coach while Charles made excuses or arrangements to not be gluing labels onto boot-polish tins for the morning. After a brief word with the coachman, they turned round and headed to the impressive stony building that held the newspaper office.

Being clandestine was almost effortless for Charles, and he spun a quick story for the clerk at the front desk about his being a messenger boy, and Mary his sister who could not be left alone, so of course she simply had to come with him, and would the clerk mind terribly pretending that she wasn't there? It was clear to Mary that Charles had rather a lot of practice at this sort of thing, and they had proceeded to the basement, with its rows of stacks of old newspapers and its disappointing dictionary.

"Now what?" asked Mary when Charles had satisfied himself that Dr Johnson's dictionary did indeed not have the word they were looking for.

"Now *that*," said Charles, pointing to a row of identical thick books in gleaming brown leather behind the counter. "*Encyclopædia Britannica*. Brand-new edition. Twenty volumes." He hopped his bottom onto the counter and swung his muddy boots over, so as not to leave a mark. *"H, I, J, K, L, M,"* he muttered, and plucked the *M* book from amongst its fellows. He placed it carefully on the counter in front of Mary and opened it slowly.

"Smell that," he said. There was something magical about the smell of oiled leather, and binding glue, and fresh paper. Mary loved books, and all hers had pages that had turned ivory, with soft edges, like childhood blankets. But this book was new, perfect, like an undiscovered country. Charles flipped through its pages methodically.

He frowned. "No mesmerism," he said, disappointed.

"What's that?" Mary asked, reading upside down.

"Mesmer, Franz. Doctor."

"Maybe mesmerism is named after him?" she suggested.

"Capital thinking!" said Charles as he read the encyclopaedia entry aloud.

Unfortunately, there was no mention of mesmerism, as far as they could tell. Dr Mesmer was apparently a scientist who believed in something called "animal magnetism" and tried to treat patients with magnets, or with buckets of water with magnets in them. This struck both Charles and Mary as odd and a little silly. But there was nothing more.

"He's dead, it says here."

Mary had a sudden thought. "When?"

"When?" Charles repeated.

"Yes, when did Dr Mesmer die?"

He scanned the entry, back up to the top.

"In 1815."

"When people die," said Mary, "they write about them in the newspaper. It's called an obituary."

"Brilliant!" exclaimed Charles, clearly excited at Mary's thinking. "It'd be over . . . there," he said, looking at the little cards with dates written on them, tacked along the bookcases. "1817 . . . 1816 . . . 1815. There we are. I'll start with December, you start with January, and we'll meet in the middle."

And so began the dull bit, sitting on the uncomfortable floor in the not-terribly-well-lit basement reading old newspapers in search of a mention of a dead doctor. From all the ink, Mary's thumbs were as black as the knocker on Newgate Prison before she reached the end of February.

Time moved at a different pace here, beneath

The Times, as they looked at days in moments, months in an hour. She had no idea how much real time had passed before she arrived, in late March 1815, at a notice about the death of poor, dead Dr Mesmer.

"Here we go," said Mary, clearing her throat. Charles shot over to her end of the bookcase and sat on the floor beside her.

"Much the same as what we already know," Mary commented. "Except this bit at the end: 'research into uncanny influence'. What's 'uncanny influence'?" she wondered aloud.

" 'Uncanny' means 'strange' or 'mysterious', and 'influence' means 'control' or 'effect'," said Charles. "So, 'uncanny influence' means 'mysterious control'."

"Or 'strange effect'. Could that be what 'mesmerism' means?" she asked.

"The whole thing might be a coincidence. Mesmerism might have nothing to do with our dead doctor and his magnets. We're guessing."

"So we have nothing," said Mary, frustrated.

"Well, we have *almost* nothing. But that's still

something," said Charles, trying to cheer her up. She smiled at him in thanks.

As they left the newspaper building, as grey as the paper itself, Mary looked at her blackened, inky thumbs. *Almost nothing is something,* she thought, and wondered what Ada would make of it all.

DISMISSED

Inky thumbs did nothing to keep the squishy balloon in Mary's chest quiet. *Peebs is a spy,* it whispered to her ribs in an oily, rubbery voice. *Oh, do shut up,* she told the balloon silently.

The first thing was to find Peebs and give him a chance to explain himself. She would help Ada accept whatever reasonable explanation Peebs could provide. Then she would tell Ada what (little) she had learned at the newspaper.

It did not surprise Mary to find the house nearly silent when Mr Franklin admitted her and took her cape. Ada was likely reading and Peebs was likely writing or planning lessons. Nodding to the ever-silent butler, she climbed the stairs to the library and found it empty of Ada. There was more nothing in the drawing room. She knocked on Ada's door. Still nothing. Curious, but hardly extraordinary. She went back downstairs, where she found it very curious that Peebs emerged, visibly shaken, from the parlour, envelope in hand.

The expression on Mr Franklin's face was curiouser still.

Something was wrong.

Peebs began buttoning his coat at the bottom of the stairs, looking pale and sad.

"Whatever's wrong, Peebs?" asked Mary. Ada was close at her heels, having come from the upstairs kitchen, bread and butter in hand. She hadn't seen the curious expression on Mr Franklin's face, but it was clear to her that Mary was upset at Peebs's being upset. Ada was momentarily proud of herself for noticing such a thing, but her pride quickly vanished in the face of concern for her friend.

"I'm afraid that I must take my leave of you." Peebs's voice was tight, and two bright red circles bloomed on his cheeks. "There has been a letter from the baroness. I have been dismissed." He cleared his throat. "Effective immediately."

Mary could scarcely breathe. She'd had no time to speak with Peebs privately about being a spy. She would be sent away to school and never see Ada again. Her mind was spinning and she knew the secret within her chest was going to explode at any second.

"What letter? Let me see it," demanded Ada.

Peebs dutifully handed her the note, folded three times and then in half, with a cracked wax seal in blood-red. Her mother's.

Ada read it aloud:

"Mr Snagsby,

It has come to my attention that you have allowed the girls under your tutelage to operate a detective agency. You may not be aware of this, as Lady Ada can be particularly clandestine in her activities, but the situation is unacceptable nonetheless. You are dismissed from service immediately, and are to send that Godwin girl off as well.

144

Please tell Lady Ada that she is to remain in the house until my return from
the country after Christmas. She shall not
receive any further visits from Mr Babbage.
And this "Wollstonecraft Detective Agency"
nonsense is at an end.

Lady Anne Isabella Byron
Baroness Wentworth"

"How could she possibly know?" asked Mary, be-
wildered.

"Her spies are EVERYWHERE!" shouted Ada,
crumpling the paper and throwing it away.

The word "spies" was too much for Mary, who
shouted "PEEBS IS A SPY!" as loudly as she could.
Ada went white as a sheet. Mary instantly regretted
her outburst.

"No, no! Not like that. He's not a spy for your
mother. He's a spy for your father!" she babbled. "I
was going to tell you but I wanted to give him a chance
to explain himself first and I never got the chance!"

Ada shook with rage.

Peebs shot Mary a hurt glance. "It is true," he admitted. "My name is not Snagsby, it's Shelley—"

"You're Percy Shelley," gasped Mary. Ada didn't know who that was.

Peebs continued. "I was a friend of your father's, Ada. Before he died, he made me promise to keep an eye on you, and serving as your tutor allowed me that opportunity. I knew your mother would never countenance my being here if she knew my real identity. I apologize for misleading you."

There was a long, strange almost-silence, like the hissing of a fuse before a bomb explodes. It was Ada, breathing in as if she were sucking through a straw. A bomb would have been quieter.

"You KNEW?" she screamed at Mary. "Peebs was a spy and you KNEW? You kept a SECRET from me? I thought you were supposed to be my FRIEND! GET OUT! ALL OF YOU! GET! OUT!" and she stormed upstairs, shaking each and every step with an expert stamp, headed no doubt all the way to the attic, and the roof.

But when she reached the top of the stairs, Mary quietly said "Ada?" in a way that made Ada turn and look down, furious and sad at once, tears welling in her eyes.

Mary simply opened her hands wide, showing

blackened thumbs. "Mesmerism. Uncanny influence" was all she said, and she uttered it with a resigned desperation. Ada could make nothing of it, and to be fair, Mary had to admit she couldn't either. Ada resumed trembling with fury and remounted her attack on the stairs, bound for her balloon.

Peebs said nothing, and could not look Mary in the eye as he left. Mr Franklin gave Mary a slow, sympathetic look, and handed her her cape, fastening it about her shoulders.

Peebs had not closed the door behind him, and Mary looked out at the steps to Marylebone Road, spattered with rain. Her heart suddenly porcelain, Mary took reluctant steps into an altogether different story, one without adventure, without clandestine names, without mystery, without uncanny influence. Without her friend.

The Wollstonecraft Detective Agency was finished.

VARIABLES

19

It was difficult to tell whether the shaking in the balloon's wicker gondola was from the wind outside or the enraged girl inside.

The space was too small to pace in, but Ada felt as though her entire body had been scooped out and filled with tigers, pacing in cages made of her hands and ribs and head. So she shook, and growled, the tigers helping her out in that way at least.

Peebs was a spy. She had thought he was useless, except for providing the odd book, but obviously he was clever enough to be a spy and had been hiding this cleverness the whole time. He could have been *interesting*. Useful. The thought frustrated her tremendously.

And Mary had betrayed her by keeping secrets. Peebs and Mary had been in—what's the word? Cahoots. They had been in cahoots, laughing at her over their little shared secret.

Perhaps Mary was a spy too! Who had sent her here, anyway? To share her tutor. Ada realized she didn't know. Could it have been her mother?

Ada growled and added her mother to her list of perpetrators: her mother who had left her in the Marylebone house with Miss Coverlet who had abandoned her and with Mr Franklin who at least never bothered her. And with Miss Cumberland who—

Huh.

That was interesting, at least. She had remembered her maid's name without even thinking about it. Ada knew she wasn't good with names that she hadn't read. Maybe . . .

No. She was going to make the Peebs cannon big enough to blast the lot of them clear across London, and they could land in a heap on her mother's doorstep in the country, and they could all be merrily dreadful together. She took out a small notebook and a pencil, to clear her thoughts.

In her notebook, she made a small lowercase *p* for Peebs. Following that with a comma, she made another small letter, this time an *m* for Mary. She put a bracket around the two letters. Thinking, she added an *a* for herself, and even a small *c* for Charles, the boy who wasn't officially there but who had placed the advertisement in the newspaper and brought their mail.

Above the brackets, she made a big *W* for Wollstonecraft, and then thought to add an *F* for Mr Franklin, who had helped by locking Peebs in the distillery cupboard. This little alphabet soup, bordered by curly brackets, calmed the tigers in the cages of her limbs.

She began another cluster of letters: an *r1* for Rebecca Verdigris, and an *r2* for Rosie Sparrow, the maid. A *b* for Beau, and an *a2* for Abernathy and an *l* for Lady Verdigris. Above all this, she placed a large *V.*

Obviously, there were some things that didn't fit in the brackets, so she made a new grouping. An *a3* for the acorn itself, and a *b2* for the fishy-smelling book. A *frh1, 2* and *3* for men in fuzzy red hats, and an *fm* for the fishmonger. Even an *o* for the omnibus that had nearly squished her flat in the road. The guard, *g,* in Newgate Prison. With each collection of brackets, she simplified all the thoughts in her head down to manageable groups, like variables in an equation.

With a red pencil, she began to make little circles: around Rebecca and Beau, around a forgotten and hastily remembered *h* for Colonel Havisham, Rebecca's dead uncle who left Rebecca the acorn in the first place. And then a line connecting Havisham with Abernathy, and then another connecting Havisham with his sister, Lady Verdigris.

She put an *X* through the guard in red pencil; he

seemed to be over with. An arrow from the three men in red fezzes leading . . . where? The exercise made her calm enough to think. Each line and letter made her breathing easier, like emptying a jumbled drawer onto the floor, sorting out piles, and only putting back the necessary things.

She could breathe again. She had her books. And she'd hardly seen Mr Babbage since all this Wollstonecraft Detective Agency business started—surely her mother wouldn't really prevent him from visiting? It was the baroness, no slouch at mathematics herself, who had encouraged Ada's love of maths in the first place. Would Mr Babbage side with her mother and stay away? Could Miss Coverlet come back? Could things just go back to the way they were before?

Ada calmed herself. She still had her balloon. She still had her books. She didn't need Mary or anyone, or even Mr Babbage, if he was going to be horrid and listen to her mother. She still had her books. Books could tell her everything she needed to know.

Like mesmerism, she thought.

If she could find a book about mesmerism, then that would prove she didn't need anyone. Books stayed put, and would not abandon her like Miss Coverlet, or that treacherous Peebs, or Mary. Or anyone in the chart of variables she had made.

She grabbed her notebook, popped open the hatch, and slid down the thick ropes to the roof, the attic and the library.

She still had her books.

NEST

20

Anna Cumberland had woken, washed and dressed before dawn. She stirred up the fire in the kitchen to make tea and warm a basin for Lady Ada, and saw to her breakfast.

There were lists for shopping, and schedules for cleaning. Putting away the autumn linens, and getting out the winter linens. There were bills from the florist, from the butcher, from the grocer and the newspaper and the fishmonger, bills for paper and candles and coal and soap and polish, all to be paid by Mr Franklin on the baroness's accounts, and all to be sorted first by Anna.

As the thin sun tinted the sky from dark grey to a lighter grey, she fetched coal and kindling and began setting the fires above stairs.

When Anna entered the library, her first thought was that of burglary. Every book was off the shelves, opened and upturned and stacked askew. The drawers were pulled from the reading desks, and the cupboards were all hanging open. But there, sprawled upon an odd and uncomfortable nest of books, slept Ada herself. No burglar, just a perfectly ordinary eleven-year-old girl genius who happened to have built herself a fort out of every single book in the library.

"Mesmerism," said Ada sleepily.

"Beg your pardon, Lady Ada?" asked Anna.

"Mesmerism. The practice of inducing a mental state in a subject of which the subject may be unaware."

"I'm sorry, Lady Ada, but I'm still not—"

"It means," said Ada, waking up, "that if you use mesmerism on someone, you can make them

do something without their even knowing they're doing it. Uncanny influence. Terribly handy. Explains everything."

"Does it, Lady Ada?"

"It does, Miss Cumberland."

Anna was so shocked at Ada's remembering her name that she nearly dropped her coal shuttle.

"Right," continued Ada, rubbing her eyes. "Much to do. First, congratulations. You wanted to be a lady's maid, and I'm not sure what that is exactly, but you are one. Starting now."

"I'm . . . Thank you, but I think the baroness—"

"Isn't here. Not until after Christmas. That's what she wrote to Peebs. Until then I'm the one with the 'lady' in front of my name, and I'm, whatsit, like the captain of a ship."

"In command?" offered Anna.

"That's it. In command. So I'll do what I want. I need you to take these envelopes to the boot-polish factory. Find a boy named Charles."

"I suspect, Lady Ada, and begging your pardon, there may be several boys named Charles at the boot-polish factory."

"Ask for one who reads. There can't be a lot of

those, and if there are, so much the better. I bet there's just the one in particular, though."

"At once, Lady Ada."

"Too many variables! That was the problem all along. I wanted to turn everything into numbers and feed them into the bleh. The bleh is the Byron—"

"Lignotractatic Engine," finished Anna.

"How do you know about the bleh?" asked Ada accusingly.

"I dust it."

"I suppose you do. But anyway, it didn't work. At first I thought I had the wrong kind of variables. People—maddeningly hard to quantify. But then I realized that wasn't the problem at all."

"No?" Anna ventured.

"No! I had *too many* variables! Two of those variables were actually the *same* variable, so I revised the equation and then it all made perfect sense!" Ada was truly excited.

"You seem truly excited, Lady Ada," said Anna cautiously.

"Of course I'm truly excited. I've been scooped out and filled with tigers. I didn't like it at first but now

I see that it's a good thing. A very good thing. And once I knew what that silly word meant . . ."

"Mesmerism," offered Anna.

"Precisely! Once I had that, well, it all just fell into place. So that means envelopes. Why are you still here?"

"Again begging your pardon, Lady Ada, but you haven't given them to me yet."

"Ah. Well, they're around here somewhere." She dug around her nest of upturned books, graphs and note scraps. "Here!" She handed a fistful of sealed envelopes, only slightly the worse for wear for having been slept on, each addressed to a different person.

"Now get out!" said Ada, in a cheerful way that seemed to erase all the anger she'd ever said it with. She said it in a way that sounded more like *Go on, unwrap your present* on Christmas morning. She said it in a way that sounded like *Let's finally have some fun around here* on a spring day. Anna nodded, a little overwhelmed by all this talk of mesmerism and variables and tigers and envelopes, and set off to find her coat and bonnet, leaving the last fires unlit.

I SUPPOSE YOU'RE
ALL WONDERING

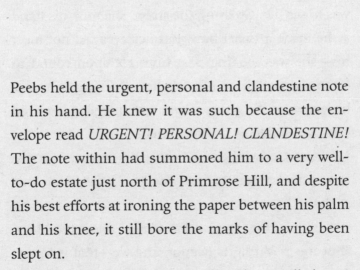

21

Peebs held the urgent, personal and clandestine note in his hand. He knew it was such because the envelope read *URGENT! PERSONAL! CLANDESTINE!* The note within had summoned him to a very well-to-do estate just north of Primrose Hill, and despite his best efforts at ironing the paper between his palm and his knee, it still bore the marks of having been slept on.

As he neared his destination, he recalled seeing a series of diagrams on the drawing-room floor

161

depicting some sort of explosive device labeled PEEBS CANNON, and briefly wondered if the summons might be some sort of trap.

His fears were set aside when he saw Mary getting out of a carriage on the other side of the road. While he had no doubt that Lady Ada was capable of constructing a cannon, he doubted very much she'd ever shoot Mary out of one, despite her anger the day before.

Mary seemed as surprised to see Peebs as he was to see her. Crossing the street, she took his hand as he made a smart bow. But her eyes did not meet his—she was looking past him. He spun round to catch sight of three red felt hats ducking behind a hedgerow, as though someone were juggling large red cans and suddenly dropped them.

"Miss Godwin," said Peebs, his attention turning to his former student, "do you know what this is about?"

"I haven't the foggiest, I'm afraid," answered Mary. "But this is Verdigris Manor, and we—that is to say, Ada and I, as the Wollstonecraft detectives—had been working on a case here."

"Then we'd best get inside."

Just as Mary's carriage pulled away, another took its place. Ada clambered out, followed by Mr Franklin, who more or less unfolded himself from the black coach like something crawling out of a beetle. Mary could see that Anna remained inside.

"Envelopes! Good," declared Ada. "Let's go."

"Go where, Ada?" asked Mary.

"Inside. I've solved the case. The whole thing." Mary had never seen Ada this excited.

"Are you sure you're feeling all right?" asked Peebs, concerned by this sudden change in Ada's mood.

Ada leaned forward to whisper loudly to Peebs, "I'm more than all right. I'm full of *tigers*." With that, she practically skipped up the stairs to the Verdigris door and let herself in, uninvited. Mr Franklin followed close behind. With a shrug, both Peebs and Mary completed the train.

The Verdigris clan, including Beau and Mr Abernathy, had assumed the same spots as on their first meeting with the Wollstonecraft girls: Rebecca was seated on the right, with Beau standing behind her; Lady Verdigris was at the head of the long, dark table, with Abernathy sort of hovering at her side. Ada saw brackets hovering in midair around both sets of people, with a *V* above the Verdigris clan and a *W* above herself and her friends.

Ada took a deep breath.

"I suppose you're all wondering why I've brought you here."

"I wasn't wondering," said Lady Verdigris. "I received a note saying it was for a school project."

"I wasn't wondering either," added Rebecca. "I received a note saying you had new information as to the missing acorn, and Rosie's innocence."

"I wasn't wondering at all," said Beau. "I received a note that there was a matter of urgent, personal and clandestine business."

"Well, I certainly wasn't wondering," said Mr Abernathy. "I received a note saying that you had an enormous fortune and required some advice on how best to manage it, and seeing as how I'm very rich, I might be able to help you."

"So, none of you are wondering?" asked Ada, disappointed.

"I'm wondering," said Mary encouragingly.

"As am I, even though I too received a note about urgent, personal and clandestine business," added Peebs, in hopes of making Ada feel better.

"Well, here it is. Beau stole the acorn," said Ada with certainty.

"Ada!" cried Mary. "We agreed to let Beau explain himself first!"

"I assure you," said Beau calmly, "I did no such thing."

"Honestly," said Rebecca, "this can't possibly be true."

Ada steeled herself. "Beau took the acorn. He just doesn't *know* he took it. It was in the book—Havisham's book. The acorn has the power of mesmerism. You can use the acorn to make people do things they wouldn't normally do, and then not even remember they did it. Uncanny influence," she added, with a nod to Mary.

There was an awkward and uncomfortable silence, so Ada added, "That's what 'mesmerism' means."

"So you're suggesting the acorn made me steal it and I don't remember?" asked Beau.

"Rosie told us she saw you take it," Ada explained. "She said you were carrying it and staring at it like something from your dreams. You were mesmerized. It explains everything."

"No, I'm quite sure it does not," said Rebecca. "Even though it means that Rosie is innocent, as

I've said all along. How could the acorn make itself be stolen?"

"Aha!" exclaimed Ada. "That was the really fun part. Taking out the variables. I had too many."

"Vegetables?" asked Abernathy.

"Variables," corrected Ada. "Parts of a problem. I thought the problem had a certain number of parts, but really, it had fewer parts. It's like putting a puzzle together with an extra piece. It doesn't fit. I had *one* puzzle piece disguised as *two* pieces."

"That doesn't make any—" started Mary.

"I know. Sorry. Full of tigers," continued Ada. "I was trying to put all these pieces together, and . . . oh, never mind. Look. Rebecca didn't steal the acorn, because she had it already. Lady Verdigris didn't steal the acorn, because she had it before and could have kept it. Rosie didn't steal the acorn, because she saw Beau Datchery take it while he was mesmerized. Plus, there was a prison guard, and three men in fuzzy red hats, and a fishmonger. That's where my secret weapon comes in."

"Secret weapon?" asked Peebs, suddenly recalling the Peebs cannon.

"Anna Cumberland, my maid," answered Ada. Mary clapped her hands with delight that Ada had finally learned Anna's name.

Just then, Anna entered the room. Abernathy began a sudden coughing fit, and turned away from the door.

"Gracious," said Lady Verdigris, "this is a most unusual school project."

"Miss Cumberland," said Ada smartly, ignoring Lady Verdigris. "Do you recognize anyone in this room?"

"I do, Lady Ada. I recognize Miss Verdigris, seated here."

"You recognize Rebecca from when she came to ask us for help," added Ada.

"Yes, Lady Ada. Plus one other person."

"Plus one other person. And whom else," Ada said, making Mary happy with the *m* in "whom", "do you recognize?"

Anna pointed at Abernathy. "Mr Flintwinch, the new fishmonger."

Abernathy gasped in pretend horror. "You are mistaken, miss. I am not a fishmonger. I am Mr Abernathy, and I'm very rich."

"Oh, you're the fishmonger all right," said Ada. "When you handed me Havisham's book, it smelled fishy. Exactly the same fishy smell that was on your fish knife, which you left at my house."

"This is ridiculous," protested Abernathy. Lady Verdigris looked sternly at him.

"Havisham 'brought home' the Acorn of Ankara from Turkey, where he was on an adventure. Only it was a national treasure, which means you can't really 'bring it home' without stealing it. And I think he stole it with *you*," accused Ada, looking straight at Abernathy. "There's a picture of you in the book. But after you helped him steal it, he gave it to his sister, Lady Verdigris, and then left it to his niece, Rebecca, in his will.

"So you pretended to be a rich friend of Havisham's. Only you're not rich. You just wanted to be close to the Verdigris family so that you could steal the acorn once it came out of the safe."

"At my birthday party," said Rebecca.

"Exactly," said Ada. "Abernathy knew about the acorn's power of mesmerism, and he used it to make Beau steal it for him. He only needed a minute alone with Beau and the necklace to make it work. Mr Datchery, do you recall such a time?"

Beau looked startled. "Well, now that you mention it, there was—"

"Of course you do," said Ada, satisfied. "Moving on."

"What would my brother—a gentleman—be doing in the company of a fishmonger?" asked Lady Verdigris.

"He's only a scoundrel who pretended to be a fishmonger. He was a sailor when he knew your brother—he's dressed like one in the picture with Havisham—and *then* when he saw his chance to get the acorn, he became a 'very rich gentleman'," declared Ada. "And he pretended to be a fishmonger after our visit so that he could sneak into the house and snoop about. Whole place smelled fishy. As a sailor, he could get fish quick as anything."

"Absurd," said Abernathy, who stuck his finger in his shirt collar, as though it were suddenly uncomfortably ill-fitting.

"But why," asked Mary, "wouldn't Mr Abernathy just run away once he had the pendant? Don't criminals usually do that?"

"He would have, but he's being followed. By three men in red fezzes. He has to find the right place and time to make his escape," answered Ada.

"Which would be now!" said Geoffrey Abernathy Flintwinch Fishmonger as he ran past Anna, skated through the entrance hall, and bolted out of the front door.

RUMBLE
AND GREAT SPEED

22

"Come on!" shouted Ada, giving chase. Mary followed.

As the girls came out of the front door, they saw the thief leap onto a carriage and roughly shove the coachman into the street. With a snap of the reins, he dashed away in the stolen vehicle.

Mary's eyes widened in amazement, and she wandered into the road, watching the carriage disappear. Suddenly her arm was seized, and she was yanked back to the steps of Verdigris Manor—just in time. The rumble and great speed of the crushing omnibus was upon the girls, and Mary was shocked to find Ada clutching her arm.

"Perfect timing! Come on!" Ada shouted once more. She ran to the back of the omnibus, as fast as her once-cherry velvet gown would allow, and leaped onto the ladder at the back. Mary, close on her heels, also jumped for the ladder, almost missing the last step.

Hand over hand, the girls climbed to the roof of the hurtling bus to see rows of benches and an assortment of men astonished at the sight of two young girls climbing onto the roof of a hurtling bus.

As carefully as they could, Ada and Mary made their way forward, gripping the backs of the pitching

benches, whipped mercilessly by the wind and a pat-
ter of new rain.

"I see him!" exclaimed Mary, pointing at the carriage ahead. "He's heading for the docks!"

"I know," said Ada, although the wind made it
impossible for Mary to hear. She tugged the back of
Mary's dress to get her to turn round, and pointed
behind them.

Following the omnibus was another carriage, and
out of its windows hung three men clutching three
red fezzes.

"Oh no!" cried Mary. "We're being followed!
Where does this bus go?"

"To the docks," answered Ada. "Hold on!"

Both girls grabbed the wet iron railing as the galloping bus turned a tight corner, and the deck bucked, tossing them about like dolls. Ancient London housefronts and warehouses fled by in a stony blur.

Mary could see the horses that were pulling Abernathy's carriage rear up and come to a stop. It seemed as though the bus were going to crash into the carriage, but the driver pulled his team of three horses up, and the girls rocked forward. Scrambling along the rain-wet deck to the rear, they found the ladder and shakily made their way down to the broad planks of the London docks.

"Tickets, please," said the bus driver, but the girls ignored him in their haste to see where Abernathy was going. As they made their way round to the front of the bus, there stood Charles with two members of the constabulary, who were clapping the thief into handcuffs.

"Well done, Charles!" shouted Ada.

"Charles?" asked Mary. "How did you know to be here?"

"Got an envelope, I did," answered Charles. "From Lady Ada. Said to wait here with the constabulary, arrest a fishmonger disguised as a gentleman, driving a stolen carriage, and wait for the two of you to arrive by omnibus."

"Ada!" said Mary, who was once again astonished. "You planned this all along?"

"I knew he'd make a run for it, and because he is a sailor, I knew he'd try to find a boat," Ada explained. "Because he is a criminal, I knew he'd steal the fastest way out, and that was the carriage. And I knew where the bus went, and when it passed by Verdigris Manor. They publish the route and schedule in the newspaper."

"You set a trap?" asked Mary.

"I set a trap."

"Good heavens, that was terribly clever of you."

"I know," Ada replied. "I mean, thank you."

Mary smiled and nodded.

Just then, a racket rose up behind the parked omnibus. Another carriage arrived, and out of it scrambled the three men in red fezzes. They quickly composed themselves and marched purposefully towards the constables, the thief, Charles and the Wollstonecraft girls. Mary felt her pulse racing in her throat, unsure of what to expect.

"Iyi akşamlar," said Ada calmly to the three men in red fezzes.

"İyi akşamlar," said the men in unison, tipping their hats with a choreographed bow.

"I believe you're looking for this," said Ada, leaning forward and plucking something from the breast pocket of Abernathy's waistcoat. Turning, she opened her hand to reveal a beautiful acorn pendant, which seemed to glow slightly in her palm even in the grey light of afternoon.

"That's mine!" yelled the thief, reaching for the jewel with his shackled hands. Ada noticed a flash of something on his forearm, a tattoo, letters. She still couldn't make them out, but this was clearly the same man who had been in her kitchen. The constables, who were waiting for a wagon to haul away their prisoner, gave him a yank on his collar, and that seemed to shut him up.

Ada carefully handed the jewel to one of the men in red fezzes, and he bowed graciously.

"Çok teşekkür ederim," he said.

"Bir şey değil," replied Ada, with a curtsy.

"What's all that?" asked Mary.

"Turkish. I learned it last night."

"You learned to speak Turkish. Last night."

"Well, I learned to read it. I've only spoken it just now."

"You are quite astonishing, Lady Ada," said Mary to her friend.

"And full of tigers." Ada smiled and took Mary's hands, giving them a squeeze. "These gentlemen are the rightful owners of the Acorn of Ankara. I noticed outside the prison that one of them was wearing a medal—I looked it up, and it's a diplomatic award from the Ottoman Empire. Turkey. Abernathy knew they were watching. That's why he didn't run away before now. But when we found him out, he didn't have much choice."

One of the befezzed gentlemen produced a velvet case. Inside was a bed of silk, and the Acorn of Ankara fitted perfectly into a small hollow. When the case snapped closed, the three gentlemen smiled and tipped their hats to the Wollstonecraft girls.

"I beg your pardon"—the bus driver approached the gathering—"tickets, please."

Mary and Ada looked at one another. "I'm afraid I don't have any money with me," said Mary.

"Me either," said Ada, checking her bag but finding only Havisham's book. "I guess I didn't think of everything."

"Perhaps I can be of some assistance," said Peebs, out of breath. With no more coaches to hire or steal, and having missed the bus, he'd run several blocks before finding a cart that took him much of the way, and then ran the rest. Huffing and puffing, he paid the bus driver, who gave a nod and returned to the monstrosity.

"Oh!" said Mary. "What of poor Rosie?"

"Charles?" asked Ada with a raised eyebrow.

"Handed it to the magistrate m'self, Lady Ada," Charles replied. "When he read that the letter was from a 'Lady Byron', he near tugged his forelock and gave the release order quick as you please."

"There you go. I presented all the evidence to the magistrate in a letter, which Charles delivered earlier. Rosie will be on her way home to Verdigris Manor as we speak."

"And did you mention in your letter to the

magistrate that you are an eleven-year-old girl?" asked Mary.

"I didn't think to bring it up. It hardly seemed relevant to the case."

"But, Ada, this is brilliant," said Mary. "You've solved the case!"

"We solved it together," said Ada. "If you hadn't pointed out that rich people don't talk about how rich they are, I never would have suspected that Abernathy wasn't really rich—or really Abernathy. And I couldn't have got to the prison, or to see Rosie, without you. So I never would have known that Rosie saw Beau take the acorn. And you and Charles found out about the uncanny influence of mesmerism."

"Together, then," said Mary, giving Ada a serious nod. "But still, I'd imagined you swooping down in your balloon with a contraption of some sort, solving all of this with science."

"But this *is* science," asserted Ada. "Wondering, guessing, trying, looking at things, sorting variables, guessing again. That's how we did it. Science."

"I say," interrupted Peebs. "Miss Cumberland and

Mr Franklin have returned to the Byron house. I suggest we do likewise."

"Agreed," said Ada. "Oh, and Peebs?"

"Lady Ada?"

"You are remissed. Or missed. Whatever the opposite of dismissed is."

"Hired, I believe," said Peebs.

"Hired, then," declared Ada. "As my tutor, so long as Mary can stay. Mother is away until after Christmas, and when she returns, she may throw you out herself if she likes. But until such time, do please consider yourself our tutor."

"I should like that very much," answered Peebs.

"Here. You can start with this." From her bag she pulled the green book with the gold acorn on the cover.

At this, the handcuffed Abernathy let out a frustrated howl. "There it is! I knew that stupid book would be a problem. I looked all over—"

But the constables gave him another sharp shake and started hustling him away along the docks.

Ada nodded, suspicions confirmed. She turned to Mary, put a finger to the side of her nose, and said, "Fishy." Then she turned back to Peebs to finish her question. "What does this mean? *De parvis grandis acervus erit.*"

"It's Latin," said Peebs. "'From small things, great things will come.' We have an English expression: 'From little acorns, mighty oaks grow.' Same meaning."

"Huh" was all Ada said. "Charles?"

Charles nodded to Ada.

"It's good to have you here, officially," she concluded.

"Thank you, Lady Ada, for a bit of excitement. It's back to the boot-polish factory for me." Charles executed a small bow and headed to work.

The girls smiled and thanked him and, hand in hand, followed Peebs to find a carriage for hire.

"Who the dickens was that boy?" asked Peebs.

And then everything went horribly wrong.

ALTITUDE

23

A huge *chuff* sent a shot of black smoke up from the water as a round-bellied steamboat chugged to life. The two constables turned towards the distraction. Abernathy, still in irons, used the cuffs to strike the first constable on the head, knocking him down, and then sharply shouldered the second constable into the river with a resounding *sploosh*.

Peebs turned at the commotion to see the thief leap aboard the little chugging boat, scramble to the wheel, and overpower the captain, tossing him overboard with the constable. Mary and Ada watched, mouths agape, as Peebs ran to the dock's edge. But Abernathy had gained control of the boat and was picking up speed.

He was getting away!

Peebs stood, frozen and frustrated. Mary watched the pistons rise and fall on the steam engine, heard the shuttle valve slam back and forth in rhythm. All the pipes and tubes reminded her of . . .

"A carriage!" cried Mary, with a plan. "Quickly!"

Peebs turned to her, puzzled.

"Trust me!" implored Mary, and Peebs put two fingers to his lips and let out the most piercing whistle the girls had ever heard. A carriage appeared as if by magic.

As fast and as dangerous as the omnibus had seemed, it was nothing compared to the banging flight of the carriage. They could hear the snap of the reins and the thundering of hooves on cobbles, and the whole thing amounted to a deafening roar of speed.

"Have you any more money with you?" shouted Mary over the racket. Ada's hands were bone white in Mary's.

"Yes, why?" asked Peebs.

"Because I promised him a pound if he'd get us back quick."

"A *pound*?" said Peebs, horrified.

"You did say alive, didn't you?" asked Ada.

A large stone beneath the carriage wheel sent the coach skyward, rattling the girls and Peebs like dice in a cup.

Moments later, bones shaken, they arrived in front of the Byron house. Fortunately, Peebs did indeed have an entire pound with him, and he handed it over to the grinning coachman as the girls practically fled the coach, across the street and up the stairs, Mary dragging Ada by the wrist like a doll through the front door.

Peebs ran in after them and saw them both run halfway up the hallway stairs, then turn back down, brushing past him to the downstairs kitchen.

"Fish knife!" yelled Mary down the hall. Peebs stepped back, and Mary and Ada once again whipped past the banister and up the stairs, this time with a wickedly sharp curved blade in Mary's hand.

"Wrench!" shouted Mary. Ada tore to her room and, after a few heartbeats of hurried rummaging, emerged with a giant wrench from under her bed.

"Balloon!" was the last battle cry needed to spur Peebs into action, and he took the stairs three at a time to catch up with the girls.

Peebs's wet shoes slid on the attic floorboards, a spatter of mud from the girls' boots having already laid a path to the window. This had been closed by Mr Franklin, and the sill was slightly swollen from rain. Mary tugged at it to get it to open, but it was no use.

"Allow me," said Peebs, who put both hands under the small half-moon of brass at the bottom and hauled with both his shoulders. The window stuttered up a bit, but held fast.

Thinking quickly, Ada plucked the fish knife from Mary's hand and thrust it into the gap between window and sill. Using it as a lever, she pushed down with all her weight, Mary joining in, as Peebs continued to pull up. After a moment of grunting and puffing, they had it open, and Ada was the first over the sill and onto the windy roof, rope firmly in hand, squinting against the rain. The others followed.

"Ada! Get in and work those ropes there! I'll untie the ones down here!" shouted Mary against the wind. "And, Peebs! Use the wrench to loosen those bolts! We need to get off the roof!"

"No!" yelled Peebs, trying to be heard above the howling of the storm and the creaking of the great ropes. "It's too dangerous! Let me go alone!"

"My balloon, my rules," said Ada with a grin. "Bolts!" And with that, she disappeared into the wicker basket. A moment later, a small side table was tossed out the top hatch, bouncing perilously off the roof and tumbling into the street below. Two chairs followed. "Now there's room for you!" she shouted in triumph.

Peebs worked on the bolted struts that connected the balloon to various chimneys—it was this tangle of pipes and funnels that had reminded Mary of the balloon when she saw the engine of the steamboat. After a few squeaks and grindings, all that connected the balloon to the roof was a single rope, and as Peebs clambered aboard, Ada sliced it neatly with the fish knife.

Mary had imagined they'd soar to the sky, but the weight of the three of them merely dropped the whole thing with a thud to the roof, where it went sliding down the black tiles like a sled on a snowy slope. A slope with a cliff at the end of it.

Peebs didn't fit completely in the basket, so his

head poked out as the balloon and basket went over the edge of the house. Mercifully, a gust of wind swept them up and over the roof of the neighbours, the gondola catching and cracking the clay of their chimney. They headed south with the wind.

"Go on!" shouted Mary to Ada.

"Go on where?" asked Ada, puzzled.

"Drive! Steer us to the river!"

"It's not made for steering, just for staying put!" yelled Ada over the wind.

Mary blinked at her. "Ah," she said. And then, "Well."

But the wind was pushing them south towards the river, which is where they wanted to go. At least, Peebs thought that was what they wanted.

"What's the plan?" he asked Mary.

"To be honest, I only got as far as this," she admitted.

"Will this float?" asked Peebs.

Ada looked down, through the sliding piles of books and rolls of paper, at the wicker at her feet and at the gaps between the wicker weave. She tried not to look too carefully as the glimpses of ground flew past at a dizzying rate.

"I doubt it," said Ada.

"I can see the docks!" cried Mary. Indeed, they were fast approaching the warehouses that lined the promenade alongside the busy river.

"There!" Ada pointed at a black pillar of soot that trudged along the Thames. Beneath that was the round-bellied steamboat, and the escaping thief. They all leaned out to look, and this had the happy effect of guiding the balloon in the steamboat's direction.

However, the balloon was descending quickly, and too sharply to clear the warehouses. At this rate, they were going to crash into the long brick buildings.

"I have a plan," said Peebs, although he wasn't entirely convinced he did. He grabbed a stout rope dangling from under the balloon's inner ring, and pulled himself up and out of the gondola, his shoes on the top of the wicker deck.

"What are you doing?" asked Mary.

"He's giving us some altitude," said Ada approvingly.

The three of them paused, taking in what Peebs was venturing to do. But the only other weight in the balloon belonged to the books, and clearly they could not be sacrificed, so the matter was settled wordlessly and with a shared shrug.

"If you'd be so kind as to calculate the timing, Lady Ada . . ." said Peebs calmly.

In her imagination, Ada turned the whole thing into a diagram. The balloon, with its altitude and weight as variables; the rate and angle of its descent and the proximity to the warehouse, Thames and target; the speed of the steamboat and the force of the wind. Simple enough.

"Ready!" said Ada, counting under her breath. "NOW!"

Peebs pushed off from the gondola, swinging on the rope like a pirate boarding a ship. With perfect timing, he stepped crisply onto the roof of the warehouse closest to the river and let go of the rope with a smart salute to the Wollstonecraft girls.

Without Peebs's weight, the balloon shot up into the sky before steadying and beginning to descend again, although more slowly this time.

"That was brilliant!" cried Mary. "Now what?"

"It's your plan, remember?" said Ada. They were

closing in on the escaping steamboat, the grey-green of the Thames looming ever closer with each wind-whipped and rain-spattered second.

The wind was pushing them southeast, but gravity was pulling them to the froth of the water, and the steamboat's wake. The closer they got to the water, the faster they seemed to go, until they were practically right on top of the boat.

Mary was sure they were going to crash, and grabbed a rope and Ada's hand, cringing. She did indeed feel a lurch, but one upward, not down. The soot and steam from the fleeing boat's engine pushed hot air into the balloon, so they hopped up and ahead of the boat, coming down again with even more force and violence.

"HOLD ON!" shouted Ada, watching the gaps between the wicker. The boat's bow came into view right in front of the toe of her boot.

The thief could not possibly have been prepared for being bashed in the head by a giant wicker basket inhabited by two remarkably clever and resourceful girls, so he wasn't. The gondola clocked him at a decent-enough speed so as to knock him out cold before it crashed into the engine, tipping the girls over sideways and spilling them to the deck. Sparks and soot flew, and despite the rain, the balloon's tattered fabric soon was in flames.

"Help me!" shouted Ada, scrambling to her feet on the slippery deck. She began pushing the basket to the deck's short railing. "If the fire spreads, the whole boat will go up!"

Ada cracked open the unsettlingly fragile basket bottom, and the pile of books spilled out like fish from a net. By now, the wicker itself was alight.

Mary rallied herself and came alongside Ada, rolling the basket, fiery balloon and all, up and over the rail, overboard into the quenching Thames. The fire was quickly out, and the basket bobbed about a bit as it took on water, and soggily sank.

Mary watched Ada watch the basket go without expression.

"I'm sorry, Ada," said Mary. She reached out and hugged Ada tightly to comfort her, although tears were trickling down her own cheeks. Ada was utterly silent for a full minute, there in the wind and rain and the puff and thump of the engine.

"We needed a bigger one anyway," said Ada at last. "And a way to steer. And," she said, looking admiringly at the steam engine, "one of *these*."

"Speaking of steering," said Mary, wiping her tears away with a smile. "Do you know how to pilot a steamboat?"

ALBÉ
AND SHILOH

Less than an hour later, the Wollstonecraft girls and their spy—*tutor,* Mary reminded herself—were once again in a carriage, but this time a slow, safe, sedate one, returning to the Byron house.

Peebs had found his way down from the roof in time to greet the girls at the dock. Through some trial and error, they had managed to guide the steamboat to its rightful spot (and captain), enabling one very sore constable and one very wet constable to once again, and with a mix of embarrassment and gratitude, take charge of their prisoner, who was still out like a snuffed candle.

They rode in silence for a moment, allowing the events of the day to settle themselves. It seemed that every variable was accounted for, every question answered. Except.

"Who are Albé and Shiloh?" asked Mary suddenly.

"I beg your pardon?" said Peebs.

"Albé and Shiloh. In the inscription in my mother's book, in Ada's library."

"Ah," said Ada. "That's how you knew he was a spy."

"That's terribly clever of you, you know," said Peebs.

"Well, you were acting suspicious in the library, so that gave me a sneaking suspicion, and I decided to investigate. But what does it mean, Albé, and Shiloh?"

Peebs smiled, first at Mary, and then at Ada. "Those were our names for each other. Ada's father, Lord Byron, and me. I called him Albé, and he called me Shiloh."

"Like Ribbon and Newdog," said Mary to Ada. "Clandestine names."

"Did you know him well?" asked Ada.

"Well enough to have, as you say, clandestine names for one another. Yes, I knew him well. He was a good friend, a brilliant man. And he would have been tremendously proud of you today."

"Mother says he was 'mad, bad, and dangerous to know'," said Ada.

"Well, he was mad, certainly. Not angry mad, but clever in a way that seemed . . . eccentric to many."

Mary flashed Ada a knowing smile.

Peebs continued. "But he was not bad. I dare say he was the best man I ever knew. As for dangerous to know, well, I must admit some truth to that. Of course, all the truly interesting people are."

Peebs reached across the carriage to take Ada's hand. "Much has been said of your father, Lady Ada, and much will continue to be said. You'll discover in time that some people are so large, so full of life, that others simply cannot help themselves from making some kind of comment. Yet that comment nearly always reveals far more about the speaker than the subject."

Ada watched Mary's face as he spoke, and saw something in the way her eyes mirrored Peebs's words—a little sad, but strong somehow. Sweet, even. She couldn't quite catch all of it.

Ada thought it must be a useful kind of cleverness to notice how people notice things. She could tell Mary was clever in this particular way, and made a note to herself to notice Mary noticing other people notice things. She could probably learn something.

"You know what else I want to know?" said Mary. "Who told your mother about Wollstonecraft? I don't see how she could have found out."

Ada shrugged. She was used to her mother knowing impossible things. "Spies. Everywhere."

"Your secret is out with more than just the baroness," added Peebs. "It was out the moment that Ada sent her letter to the magistrate. It won't be long before half of England knows about the Wollstonecraft detectives."

"It can't be as bad as all that," Mary objected. "One magistrate, two constables and the baroness? I'm sure we're still quite clandestine."

Peebs was unconvinced. "Never underestimate the power of a good secret, hungry for the telling. While it may be the grandest city in all the world, London is a village as far as gossip is concerned."

Just then, Ada froze. Something clicked in her

brain, like the spindles of the bleh, although she didn't know what it meant.

"Ada?" asked Mary. "Are you all right?"

"I don't know. I'm not certain. I may have missed . . . something."

"About the case?" said Mary. "I can't imagine what. The acorn is in the hands of its rightful owners, Rosie's out of prison, and the criminal has been apprehended. The constables are at Verdigris Manor now, explaining everything."

Ada nodded slowly in agreement. It all added up neatly.

"And yet," said Ada, staring out the window, "our thief doesn't strike me as the very cleverest of criminals."

"It seemed like a very clever crime to me," said Peebs.

"And I have no doubt Mr Abernathy will be in the newspaper tomorrow, where he belongs," said Mary.

It pleased Ada to think he undoubtedly would.

And yet.

SISTERS

25

The carriage containing Ada, Mary and Peebs arrived safe and sound at the Marylebone house, which now seemed plain without its comical balloon hat. Mr Franklin stood by the open door, taking the girls' capes and bonnets as they entered. There was the smell of baking, and the marble of the floor was gleaming, freshly mopped. A kettle whistled in the upstairs kitchen, only to have its shriek spin down to a sigh as it was taken off the stove. Mary breathed deeply of the house she had been sure she'd never see again—first from banishment, and then from balloon crash.

Peebs excused himself to attend to the drawing room, and the girls marched upstairs to take their tea in the miraculously restored-to-order library.

Cosy in the familiarity of books, Mary reached for the stack of letters that had been placed upon the small reading table, presumably by Mr Franklin.

"No, leave those," said Ada. "That's enough for today, I should think."

"Oh, they're not all from the newspaper," said Mary, rifling through the envelopes. "There's something here from Rebecca."

"Mmm?" asked Ada.

Mary cracked open the seal. "It's a wedding invitation," she said, delighted.

"Mmm," replied Ada, indifferent.

"Oh, something else too. One for you, and one for me."

Ada couldn't recall getting letters, except the occasional dressing-down from her mother. She reached for the paper, noticing carefully the unfamiliar writing as she unfolded the note.

"Good heavens," said Mary, at her letter.

"Good grief," said Ada, at hers.

"My sister," said both girls together.

"My stepsister, Jane, actually," explained Mary. "It seems she's on her way—right now—to join us as a Wollstonecraft detective. She says something about it being a perfect opportunity to meet the right sort of people in society."

"My half-sister, Allegra," added Ada, "says she was going to run away from the convent to join the circus, but when she thought about how angry my mother would be, she decided to run away here and be a detective instead."

There in the heart of the Marylebone house, a hundred sounds from all of London reached them ever so faintly through the windows: the cawing of crows, the shouting of vendors and merchants, the cries of babies unwilling to nap, the barking of dogs one to another across Regent's Park and down Baker Street. But in that instant, all sound fell away, except for the clatter of an arriving carriage, and then another.

Eyes wide, the girls leaped to their feet and nearly slid down the stairs to the front door and opened it.

Ada saw two girls step out of two separate carriages

in unison. The first girl was about Mary's age, pale with a mass of curly hair piled up fashionably high on her head, walking elegantly towards the house. A step behind her was a girl of about nine, half running; a wiry and sun-bronzed girl with her clothes in disarray. Ada wondered if she herself looked like such a wild thing, from a distance.

Mary was unsure as to what to say, and even more unsure as to what Ada would do. It was exactly this sort of sudden change that often made Ada incendiary.

Standing there on the doorstep, Ada continued to look off into the distance. She breathed deeply and pulled back her shoulders, standing tall under the portico before speaking.

"We're going to need more crime."

NOTES

1826

The year 1826 itself is practically a character in the book. John Quincy Adams was president of the United States. The prince regent of England had become King George IV just six years before, and the future Queen Victoria was only seven years old. By 1826, the world had seen a recent flurry of inventions: Volta's electric battery (1800), Fulton's submarine and torpedo (1800), Winsor's patented gas lighting (1804), Trevithick's steam locomotive (1804), Davy's electric arc light (1809), Bell's steam-powered boat (1812) and Sturgeon's electromagnet (1824). It was an exciting time of technological advancement, and it brought forth two very bright girls who changed the world through their intellect and imagination.

The lives of women—and particularly girls—were extremely limited and under constant watch. Women were not allowed to vote or practise professions, and were widely thought to be less capable than men. A girl's value to her family was in her reputation and her service, and she was expected to obediently accept a husband of her parents' choosing. Any threat to that reputation—like behaving unusually—was often enough to ruin a family.

However, because a girl was not expected to have a career and compete with her (or anybody's) husband, upper-class girls were free to read or study as they wished, for few took them seriously. Because of this rare freedom, the nineteenth century saw a sharp surge in the intellectual contributions of female scientists and mathematicians, with Ada foremost among them.

ADA

AUGUSTA ADA BYRON (1815–1852) was a brilliant mathematician and the daughter of the poet Lord Byron (who died when Ada was eight). Largely abandoned by her mother, she was raised by servants (and sometimes her grandmother) at the Marylebone house and was very much cut off from the world as a child.

With her legendary temper and lack of social skills (a modern historian unkindly calls her "mad as a hatter"), Ada made few friends. Her mother insisted that young Ada have no connection to her father's friends or even his interests, so Ada turned to mathematics. She worked with her friend Charles Babbage on the tables of numbers for Babbage's "Analytical Engine"—a mechanical computer—which was not built in his lifetime. But Ada's contribution to the work, as well as her idea that computers could be used not only for mathematics but also for creative works such as music, has caused many people to refer to her as the world's first computer programmer. Babbage called her the Enchantress of Numbers. She really did have an interest in mesmerism.

Ada grew to control her temper and insecurities and, at nineteen, was married to William King, a baron who became the Count of Lovelace three years later. This is why Ada is more commonly known as Ada Lovelace. She had three children—Byron, Annabella and Ralph—and died of cancer at the age of thirty-six. She continues to inspire scientists and mathematicians to this day, and many worthwhile projects are named after her.

MARY WOLLSTONECRAFT GODWIN (1797–1851) was the daughter of the famous feminist writer Mary Wollstonecraft (who died ten days after giving birth to Mary) and the political philosopher William Godwin. William Godwin married Mary Jane Clairmont in 1801, and Mary grew up in a mixed household of half siblings and stepsiblings in Somers Town, in north London. She read broadly and had an appetite for adventure and romanticism. She ran away with Percy Shelley at age sixteen, and over one very famous weekend with Shelley, Lord Byron (Ada's father) and the early vampire novelist Dr John Polidori, Mary came up with the idea for the world's first science-fiction novel, *Frankenstein; or, The Modern Prometheus,* which she wrote at age nineteen.

In real life, Mary was eighteen years older than Ada—old enough to be her mother. But I thought it would be more fun this way—to cast these two luminaries as friends.

PERCY BYSSHE (rhymes with "fish") SHELLEY (1792–1822) was an important poet and the best friend of Ada's father, Lord Byron. Percy came from a wealthy family, and he offered to support Mary's father and the Godwin family. At age twenty-two, he ran off with sixteen-year-old Mary to Switzerland, and they were married two years later. He drowned at the age of twenty-nine when his sailing boat sank in a storm.

While in reality Peebs had died even before our story begins, I have extended his life so that he, Ada and Mary can be in this story together. It is Peebs, as Ada's father's friend and Mary's future husband, who provides a real-life link between our two heroines.

ANNE ISABELLA NOEL BYRON (1792–1860) was the wife of Lord Byron, and Ada's mother. Extremely intelligent and well educated, she was an accomplished mathematician in her own right. Her marriage to Byron was difficult, and he left her shortly after Ada was born. It wasn't actually the baroness who first called Ada's father "mad, bad, and dangerous to know", but that does describe her feelings towards him. She became very religious and very strict, and she found Ada too much like her father, calling Ada "it" in letters to Ada's grandmother. She was not all bad, though. She committed much of her life to antislavery causes and prison reform. And she nursed Ada through the illness that eventually killed her.

MARY WOLLSTONECRAFT (1759–1797) was an early feminist writer most famous for *A Vindication of the Rights of Women,* in which she argued for education and equality for all girls. She lived in Paris during the French Revolution and was a friend of, and correspondent with, many leading intellectuals of the day, including Thomas Paine. She later wrote *Original Stories from Real Life,* the children's book that Mary finds in the Byron library in our story. Mary Wollstonecraft married the political philosopher William Godwin, and she died from complications following the birth of her second daughter, Mary.

GEORGE GORDON BYRON (1788–1824) was Ada's father and a famous poet of the romantic movement. He rejected many of the ideas of his time, particularly about love, marriage, the roles of the rich and the poor, religion, and being a "responsible adult" in general. He was a man of many love affairs, huge debts, heroic acts, occasional cruelty, and terrible sadness. He was born with a deformed foot that was very painful through his whole life, but he was a capable boxer, horse rider and swimmer. He travelled throughout Europe into Persia and the Ottoman Empire. At the time, Greece was under the control of the Ottomans, and despite not having military experience, Byron led a force of Greek rebels against the Turks. During the military campaign, he became ill and died of fever.

A brooding, tragic and noble figure, Byron likely inspired the character of Dracula in Bram Stoker's classic novel. He never knew his children, Ada and Allegra, having abandoned Ada to her mother and Allegra to nuns.

CHARLES

CHARLES DICKENS (1812–1870) is considered one of the great writers of Victorian England. He really was fourteen in 1826, and he really did work in a boot-polish factory gluing labels. He loved books and was a keen observer of everyday life in London. The description of Newgate Prison in this story comes from his *Sketches by Boz* (1836). Other names in this book come from his writings: Flintwinch, Datchery, Havisham, Snagsby—even Chuzzlewit. He is best known to young readers as the author of *A Christmas Carol*. The bit about the carriage and pretending not to be there is made up, although he was certainly clever enough and cheeky enough to have got away with it.

CHARLES BABBAGE (1791–1871) was an English inventor, engineer and mathematician who designed the first mechanical computer. Though he worked with Ada Byron to develop the mathematical models that would make the machine work, it wasn't built until over a century after his death. He really was a friend of Colonel Sir George Everest, who came back from India with philosophical ideas about mathematics.

NEWGATE PRISON

First built in the twelfth century, the prison was destroyed in the Great Fire of London in 1666 but rebuilt in 1672. Daniel Defoe, author of *Robinson Crusoe,* was imprisoned there, as was Captain Kidd, the notorious pirate. It was truly a terrible place and was taken down in 1904. The expression "as black as Newgate's knocker," referring to the prison doors' heavy iron rings, was popular in the nineteenth century.

MESMERISM

The word "hypnotism" didn't exist in Ada and Mary's time, but "mesmerism" means the same thing. Magnetism wasn't really understood by the scientists of the day, and so it was used to describe any kind of influence on something without touching it. Specifically, mesmerism was about "animal magnetism", an "uncanny influence" on people (and presumably animals).

THE MOONSTONE

An 1868 novel by Wilkie Collins, *The Moonstone*, is often considered to be the first detective novel written in English (although Edgar Allan Poe had already written some short detective stories). Our mystery is a nod to some of the elements of this classic: an heiress receives a jewel as a birthday present from her uncle—an adventurer now dead—only to have it stolen, with the lady's maid confessing to the crime. I thought it would be fun to have the world's first computer programmer and the world's first science-fiction author solving the world's first fictional detective mystery.

THE SISTERS: JANE AND ALLEGRA While we'll
find out more about these new girls in Book Two,
Mary really did have a stepsister, Jane (who would
later be known as Claire), and Ada really did have a
half sister, Allegra. As with Mary, Jane's timeline is
moved so that she can be young alongside Mary and
Ada. In real life, Allegra died of fever at age five, so I
have extended her life in this series, as I felt rather
sorry for her.

THANK YOU

Thanks to the many kind people who supported my Kickstarter campaign and gave this project momentum: Niki Whiting and Adam Blodgett; Steve Turnbull; Phoebe Reading; Charles Alvis; Amanda Zoellner and Bryan Fink; Dave Griffith; Geoff, Melissa, and Daniel Tidey; Shoshana and Amelie Reed; Bill Hovingh; Elaine Barlow; Matthew Mattei; Atlee and Benjamin Sharpe; Heidi Berthiaume; Laura and Alyssa Gluhanich; Jason Driver; Mike Firoved; Lawrence McAlpin; Jenny Jacob; Cyd Harrell; Lynda Forman; Michael, Eliza and Juliet Quinn; Jocelyn Scheintaub; Mara Georges; Jason Stevens; Jason Roop; Martha and Peter March; Wilma Jandoc; Jessica; Chris Coyier; Agnes Ponthus; Wanda L. Anderson; Karine; Melia and Ryanne Gordon; waipo5; Kathryn Blue; Brian McCormick; Paul

Hedges; Ingrid; Roelof Botha; Mathew and Annika Kayley Beall; Bryce Platt; Andy Flood; Tracy Ann and MaCaybreh Daily; Cindy, Sophie, Konrad and Anna Zawadzki; Megan; Sabine Schoenbach; Stephanie McMillen Sherry; Colin Samuels; Nawaf Bahadur; Eileen Chow; Jen Sparenberg; Tracey Gaughran-Perez; Dan Romanelli; Robin Borelli; Mark, Sabrina, and Zoey Taraba; David and Kashi McKellar; Tony Lamair Burks II; Carolyn and Nick Atkins; Julia, Isabella, and Grace Arrese; Alexander Cheng-Chien Yao; Shannon and Anais Hammock; the Edwards family of Narberth, Pennsylvania; James, Connie, Katherine, and Angelica Hall; Maura Donohue; Ryder, Hayden and Lane Lack Daniels; Mock; Glenn Slotte; Jorge Zamora; Bruno Maitre; Charles Hansen; Aaron, Bethany and Alexander Reiff; Joy Lock; Tanja Norwood; Margaret Sheer; Benjamin Listwon; Alan Salisbury; Kim Worsencroft; Mike Smith; Mary Rose Mueller; Deborah Goldsmith; Felomena Li; Christine Hatfield; Taroh Kogure; Mark Reynolds; Naer Chang; Kassandra and Sammie Jo; Warren Cheung; Bing; Rosie; Lee Ann Farruga; Nadia Cornier White; Deanna Jones; Joseph Goethals; Jonathan Cameron; Niki Tan; Dave Hoover; Daniel Abraham;

Susan Standiford; Kristophor Bex; Cameo Wood; Jean Teather; Matt Brooks; Roger Hoffmann; Matthew Oliphant; Micheal Hoffa.

Thanks also go out to Team Wollstonecraft: Zandra and Claire and Kevin and Aimee; to Xoe and Sebastian, who left Daddy alone for five more minutes just ten more minutes just one more minute I promise; to my agent, Heather Schroder, at Compass Talent in New York for agreeing to champion the Wollstonecraft girls through the baroque and byzantine world of mainstream publishing; and to Nancy Siscoe for her myriad insights and contributions, for finding a home for this series—as it continues to evolve—at Knopf, and for sending me off in fascinating fact-checking directions.

JOIN THE

WOLLSTONECRAFT
DETECTIVES

ON THEIR NEXT CASE!

❧

Turn the page for a sneak peek at Book Two,
The Case of the Girl in Grey.

GHOST GIRL

Mary's stepsister Jane had first embarrassed her on their morning carriage rides to the Byron House by asking Charles (the boy behind the book) why he was there, and if he was being ungentlemanly and (she stressed the word) *antisocial* by reading in front of them.

Charles, as Mary had expected, handled himself expertly, although his answer was too direct for Jane's taste: Charles had no money for a carriage, but he traded with the coachman for a ride to work, which gave him a moment's peace to enjoy his book, so long as he pretended he wasn't there and nobody minded.

"Which we don't," Mary assured him. "Mind, that is. Not at all."

Jane had further embarrassed Mary by insisting on calling Charles "Master Dickens", something Mary then realized she ought to have been doing all along.

After the first week of carriage rides, Jane had settled into the routine, and aside from what struck Mary as an overly formal "Good morning", Jane had kept largely to herself, immersed in her own book.

The carriage turned from their home on Polygon Road down Eversholt Street, seemingly in the wrong direction, only to turn again the right way some minutes later. This turn took them towards the outer circle of Regency Park proper, its manicured green all around them.

Without warning, the carriage rocked back, bucking the girls nearly into Charles's lap, and Mary's knee landed hard on the rough wooden planks. The horses cried out in front, hooves hammering the autumn-wet road.

"Are you both unhurt?" asked Charles, offering a hand. As they nodded and righted themselves, Mary opened the carriage door to see what was the matter, and in the grey of the sky and the road and the rain, she caught a glimpse of a girl, perhaps a little older than herself, in a grey shift, soaking wet and shivering.

"It's a madwoman!" shouted the coachman in the rain. "She ran in front of us like the devil were on her heels! Nearly ran 'er to 'er death, we did!" Mary didn't hesitate, but shot after her, with Charles not long behind—but another carriage bolted past, cutting him off from Mary's pursuit.

The grey girl fled alongside a hedge bordering an important-looking building of white stone, before disappearing into some trees. Mary ran after her until all was a blur: the green hedge, the white stone, the grey girl.

"Wait!" shouted Mary at the vanishing girl. "Are you all right?"

Mary leaned a gloved hand against a tree to catch her breath. A pale-faced girl peered out from behind another tree, a short distance on, auburn hair tangled and rain-pasted to her cheeks.

"I say," panted Mary. "I do hope you're all right. You've had a bit of a fright, I should think."

"No," replied the girl, as though from a great distance. "I'm not all right." There was a strange, otherworldly note in her voice.

Mary was alarmed. "Was it the horses? Were you hurt?"

"No," came the reply. "It wasn't the horses. I'm just not all right."

"Please do come back to the carriage. Out of the rain. You're soaked through. We can take you home."

"I'm not all right," said the girl in grey. "And I'm not going home." With that, she turned an even whiter shade of pale and fled into the forest alongside the path, quick as a bird.

Mystified by the disappearing girl's odd behaviour, Mary paused, unsure of what to do. Charles caught up with her at last.

"Miss Godwin? Are you altogether well?" he enquired. "You look as if you've seen a ghost."

"Perhaps I have, Master Dickens." Mary adjusted her bonnet and pulled her cape against the rain as she gave Charles a nod of thanks. "Perhaps I have."

TRITHEMIUS

Up in the library, burrowed in a book, Ada heard the lion's-head knocker, the sounds of doors and the fetching of trays: all the formalities of "visitor". Ada's list of approved visitors had a single name on it, and as she was quite sure that this name did not belong to whomever Mr Franklin had deposited in the downstairs parlour, she didn't feel the need to investigate.

Until, of course, she heard a flurry of light footsteps on the stairs. Allegra was on her way to investigate, and Ada knew she ought to head her off.

Mr Franklin loomed at the bottom of the stairs

in such a fashion that Allegra was unable to find her away round him. He blocked her path until Ada, relatively composed, was behind her. The butler then pivoted like a hinged door, directing their attention to Anna, Ada's maid, as she emerged from the parlour. Anna smiled and bobbed a quick curtsy.

"Lady Ada, there's a Mrs Mary Somerville to see you."

Ada froze. "That's impossible," said Ada. "It can't be."

"You were expecting her. She sent a note."

"A note?"

"You read it at breakfast, Lady Ada."

"I don't remember it. I would have remembered it."

"You were reading something else at the same time," added Anna.

"I can do that! I can read two things at the same time and remember them."

"I'm sure you can, Lady Ada."

"I would have remembered a note from Mrs Somerville!"

"No doubt, Lady Ada."

"Mary Somerville. The cleverest person in England. The smartest, cleverest person in the whole world. Wrote me a note. I would have remembered."

"As you say, Lady Ada," said a patient Anna.

Allegra. The sister had entered Ada's brain like a mosquito in a summer night's bedroom. She was sure she would have remembered everything if her sister hadn't simply . . .

Allegra trotted into the parlour like a spaniel, not caring a bit who Mrs Somerville might be, or that she wasn't there to visit the younger sister.

Ada, in something of a shock, followed.

A kindly woman in a coffee-brown dress rose and extended her hand. She was perhaps thirty-five or so, with a prominent nose and slightly slanty eyes. Her plain façade could not mask a ferocious intelligence, which Ada recognized at once.

"Lady Ada," said the woman. "Delighted to meet you at last."

Ada froze once more, starstruck. She blinked forcefully, and as this didn't help, she blinked again. The woman continued.

"I'm—"

"Mary Somerville."

"Yes, that's right. I understand we have a mutual friend in—"

"Mr Babbage," Ada interrupted again.

Mrs Somerville smiled, and her eyes motioned to

the furniture in the subtlest reminder that they might all wish to sit down.

"Trithemius," Ada added, blinking yet again.

"I beg your pardon?" asked Mrs Somerville.

"*Steganographia.* 1499. I have your—I mean—Mr Babbage left—gave me—I—you—"

"Have I startled you, Lady Ada?" asked Mrs Somerville, concerned.

Ada continued to stare at Mrs Somerville, and Allegra stared at Ada, trying not to laugh.

Ada panicked and bolted from the room, leaving Allegra to hurl herself at the couch and begin chatting away at the now-captive Mrs Somerville.

Ada shot to the library, found her quarry, and flew back down the stairs to find Mary, looking soggy and pale, in the foyer with the curly-haired and perfectly dry Jane in tow.

"What's wrong?" asked both Ada and Mary of each other at once.

"I'm fine," said Mary. "Our carriage had a bit of a start. Well, a stop would be more accurate. But what about you? You look a shambles. How did you get so sooty?"

Ada was still wide-eyed and flustered.

"Mary Somerville. In my house. Behind that door. Trapped, with Allegra."

Mary knew that when Ada began to chop up her sentences, she was feeling overwhelmed.

"Dear Ada, do calm down. Now, are you saying that Allegra has trapped some woman behind the door, and we are to set her free?"

"No, no. It's Mary Somerville. She's the cleverest person in England. She's the cleverest person in the *whole world*." Ada's words were racing. "Honestly, she's so clever they had to invent a new word for it."

"What word?" asked Mary.

"Scientist!" Ada babbled excitedly. "They used to say 'men of science' until she came along. And I have her book—well, I have several of her books. The ones she's written. But I mean Mr Babbage's book, well, he didn't write it, Trithemius wrote it three hundred and twenty-seven years ago. But Mary Somerville wrote in it! And I read her notes! And there are things I don't understand! It's probably the best thing that's ever happened."

ABOUT THE AUTHOR

Jordan Stratford has been pronounced clinically dead, was briefly (but mistakenly) wanted by Interpol for espionage, and has won numerous sword fights. He now lives on a tiny, windswept island in British Columbia, Canada, with his wife and children.

Jordan's passions for history, science, maths and literature come together in this series. He is particularly eager to shine a light on some of the pioneering and underappreciated women in those fields, and to inspire girls to dream big, change the world, and laugh really hard. You can read more about the world of Wollstonecraft at WollstonecraftAgency.com.

ABOUT THE ILLUSTRATOR

Kelly Murphy is an accomplished picture-book and fiction author and artist. She is a graduate of the Rhode Island School of Design, where she now serves on the faculty. Her many acclaimed books include the Beastologist series by R. L. LaFevers and *The Mouse with the Question Mark Tail* by Richard Peck. Kelly lives with her husband in New England. You can read more about her work at kelmurphy.com.